HUDSON RUN

J.E. KROSS

COPYRIGHT © 2009 BY J.E.KROSS

THIS IS A WORK OF FICTION. NAMES, CHARACTERS, BUSINESSES, PLACES, EVENTS AND INCIDENTS ARE EITHER A PRODUCT OF THE AUTHOR'S IMAGINATION OR USED IN A FICTITIOUS MANNER. ANY RESEMBLANCE TO ACTUAL PERSONS LIVING OR DEAD, OR BUSINESSES, OR ACTUAL EVENTS IS PURELY COINCIDENTAL.

DEDICATION

FOR ALL OF MY RAILROAD BROTHERS AND SISTERS:

I DEDICATE THIS TO YOU,

YOUR FAMILIES AND FRIENDS.

MOSTLY, TO OUR BROTHERS AND SISTERS WHO HAVE PASSED ON BEFORE US, THEIR SHED BLOOD ON EVERY LINE A HAUNTING, WHISPERING REMINDER OF OUR RAILROADS PAST, PRESENT AND …THOSE UNSPOKEN THINGS WE'VE ALL LEARNED ALONG THE WAY.

-J.E.KROSS

CHAPTER 1

"Jackie—I can't," Sheri groaned in the darkness.

"We have no choice," the Conductor snapped at her assistant and then pulled her body closer to the boxcar's loading door.

She propped Sheri up next to the huge opening on the side of the baggage car as the mammoth train raced over the rails, looked pensively for a moment at her injured Assistant, and then closed her eyes.

Jackie reluctantly reopened them, turned, and began to walk through the hollow boxcar toward the engine, tightening her ponytail as she went.

"This is *nuts*, that's what this is," she grumbled as she took a deep breath and pulled open the boxcar's end door. The wind pushed it past her, smashing it on its hinges against the inside wall of the car. Holding on tightly to the grab iron in the doorway, she looked the short distance across to the back end of the engine and shook her head nervously. Carefully, she crossed her left leg over and straddled between the ledges that separate the locomotive from the train. The wind whipped her face as she brought her other foot forward and stood pressed up against the back of the engine. The *whoosh-whooosh-whoosh* of the train barreling past buildings that she heard from the comfort of the inside of the baggage car was now a loud and intimidating *wisp-wisp-wisp*.

Jackie quickly reached over and tightly gripped the handle on the outside rear corner of the engine. As the train thundered to one hundred and thirty miles per hour, she inched her way over to the corner and lowered herself onto the metal stirrup. Then she locked her right elbow around the handle and reached down, pulling up on the metal uncoupling lever. The pin that ran between the knuckles that held the cars together rose; Jackie's heart skipped a beat, knowing there was definitely no turning back.

TWO DAYS EARLIER

    As the Conductor drove farther away from the city limits and began to wind up around the mountain road through a tunnel of fall foliage, she loosened her tie and undid the top button of her white dress shirt. Putting the nineteen-ninety-something black Chevy on cruise, she leaned back in the seat. Almost at the top of the mountain, she took a right-hand turn down the long, gravel driveway and, noticing a green Chevy parked in front of her garage, stopped the car abruptly. Something wasn't right.

    Jackie hadn't had a single visitor since the divorce over three months ago - except, of course, for Sheri.

Living alone now, she decided caution was the best policy and pulled in behind Steve's abandoned Ford pick-up, directly across from the stranger's Malibu.

The September dusk shot pink and orange rays through her car as she grabbed the palm-size can of pepper spray from under the driver's seat and stepped out into the driveway.

Squinting, she walked toward the scrawny yet ridiculously large-headed man sitting between two of the white columns on the massive front porch. "*Better not be,*" she muttered to herself, noticing that he was beginning to resemble the man she had thrown off the train (to cheers) a few days ago at the Rhinecliff station. Approaching cautiously, she placed the can of pepper spray in the back waistband of her Levi's™.

He was smiling at her. "Hi," he said. "Are you Jackie McKeon?"

It wasn't him. Good.

"That's me," Jackie responded curtly. "Publishers Clearing House, right?" she quipped.

The smile left his big, round face as he stood up and held out a manila envelope.

"You've been served," he said flatly.

Jackie took the envelope. "Served?" She looked down at it briefly and then watched the man make his way across the grass back to his car, shaking his head.

"I'd ask ya out," he said, continuing toward the car, "but this isn't the best 'how we met' story in the world."

"Gee, thanks," she replied, fishing her keys from her jeans pocket. She watched him pull out of the driveway as he took a bite out of what appeared to be a large candy bar.

Perplexed, Jackie opened the front door. Rubbing the scar tissue on her palms, she contemplated: The divorce was final, and there were no children involved.

She set the envelope on the black cast-iron table in the foyer, took the pepper spray out of her back waistband, set it next to the envelope and headed for the kitchen.

Grabbing a can of soda from the stainless-steel refrigerator, then a glass, Jackie walked over the Italian-marble tile through the foyer and picked up the envelope again. Moving into the living room, she set the glass on the coffee table. Popping the tab on the soda, she scanned the papers inside--and froze.

The letters were large and menacing. Jackie read the first two words over and over again, her mind unable to comprehend.

"Foreclosure Notice," she murmured in shock, and then read it again. "Fore-clo-sure. WHAT?!" she screamed. The echo shot through the expansive living room like lightning on a hot summer night.

The Conductor tried to read the notice but couldn't. Dropping it onto the table, confusion racing through her veins, she felt her head begin to pound.

Fifteen years she'd put into the home, and calling the house a home was generous to say the least. Sheri could never understand how Jackie could have rebuilt it, let alone endured living in it at all. Yet she continued, as if possessed into believing that constantly working on it could bring them back somehow.

Every cent she'd ever earned--everything since she was fifteen years old with a paper route--had been sucked into her obsession.

Her thoughts quickly returned to the divorce, the mortgage...the mistress.

"*Joint account*," she whispered uneasily, looking down at the papers; her stomach became queasy. "*Steve…*"

She took a long drink of the soda, gaze fixed on the notice on the table.

It wasn't enough that Steve--who exercised less control over his zipper than a certain golfer--had ruined her faith in men. Now he was trying to take away the only solid memory of *them* she had: the house, or The Castle, as Sheri referred to it. She sat motionless, staring into the empty stone fireplace as though it were a portal. Her eyes reddened as she took another gulp of the soda, glass forgotten. The sun had set and the light began to empty from the room, yet she remained there, paralyzed.

Distantly, as if miles away, she could still hear her mother's screams. And when the silence came, her innocence would be replaced with something much darker.

Rebuilding the house had become her fixation when she was just a young girl staring at the mountain of charred ruins that remained of it.

Palms that had once held Barbies and multicolored Play-Doh™ were forever branded with the scars from trying to drag her mother's horrific remains out of the burning second-floor bedroom with her tiny, six-year-old hands.

She had spent her entire childhood rebuilding her family's home in her mind, as though her parents might reappear if she got it right. It had taken a lifetime's worth of dedication and perseverance to make the reconstruction a reality. Everything—down to the last nail --all of it had been chosen and placed by her hand. No one had the right to take it from her, least of all that philandering loser she'd called a husband for a time.

Reluctantly, she reached under the coffee table's glass top and retrieved the newspaper article. It was lodged, preserved, within the pages of Webster's dictionary, somewhere between *abandoned* and *arson*. Sheri had drunkenly made that observation, and then suggested shoving it between *shit* and *syphilis* instead, but, with a pounding headache the following morning, had apologized.

"There's no way, Steve," Jackie said aloud. Her face flushed with anger as she picked up the notice and finally began to read it.

Her eyes began to widen as she read. Biting down hard on her bottom lip, she set the papers on the coffee table, her eyes stinging with tears.

"How could you--*you bastard*," she whispered into the darkening room.

Her pulse quickened as she got up from the couch and stormed across the room. Grabbing her cell, she scanned the contacts, selected Steve, and waited. Answering machine. *Bastard.*

"How could you—you're a thief," she seethed into the phone. Then stopped short, shaking her head.

She closed her eyes, and then gently set her cell phone down. She walked back over to the table and picked up the notice. Taking a small sip of the soda, hands shaking, she continued to read.

The account was twenty grand in arrears, her credit undoubtedly destroyed. She knew instantly Steve's bank buddy had had a hand in this. She took a deep breath and put the notice back into the envelope while looking with guilt at the aged article. She picked it up, gently gliding her fingers over the text, and then returned it to Webster's waiting pages.

The house, not counting utilities, came to just over eighteen hundred dollars a month. On her salary, she was left with just enough to survive. But Jackie never cared much about money or lobster tails. For her, it was all about the house; it was always about the house. Steve hated her for that, but could never change it.

Financially, whenever things were tough, she reluctantly conjured the memory of her father's car squealing into the driveway that monstrous night so many years ago, and of him rushing to her mother's charred body. Jackie saw him holding her and rocking her gently, a shocked look on his face as he watched their family's home go up in flames—and heard the sickening sound her mother's hard, burnt skin made as he rocked her. Skimming a glance down over the floor, Jackie remembered the last words her father had spoken to her before she found him hanging from the shower stall in the dirty hotel, then closed her eyes. She could feel their ghosts returning in the darkness.

Her mind often filled with such ghastly images, so excruciating that if revealed to the light of day a good mother would surely shield her child's eyes from them. But they were inside of her, and would come and go as they pleased.

Jackie rose from the couch, stripping off her T-shirt and socks, throwing them on the kitchen floor as she passed through into her den.

Turning on the computer, she decided to visit an online chat room, not so much to chat herself but to escape the ghosts for a moment, to "listen" to a conversation, any conversation.

Before long, she found herself in one of her own. And although it wasn't the first time Jackie had tried to chat online, she decided this would definitely be the last. Staring at the computer screen, she rubbed her forehead uneasily.

The house was dark, empty, and--except for the lone cricket lurking around--completely quiet. Shaking her head in disbelief, she turned off the computer and sat there speechless a moment more, face flushed.

"Pervert," she mumbled at the computer, then walked back through the house to the foyer, grabbed the can of pepper spray off the cast-iron table, and then made her way upstairs to the bedroom. The chilly evening air had settled into the house; she pulled the peach-colored goose down up snugly around her bare shoulders, her eyes feeling puffy and tired.

"What the hell was wrong with that guy?" she whispered into the darkness, eyes finally closed, brows still furrowed. Within a few moments, Jackie McKeon was asleep.

CHAPTER 2

On the other side of town, Sheri Daniels was awoken by a piece of paper caught in the enormous square fan at the foot of her bed, which Jackie had appropriately dubbed The Crop Duster.

Climbing out of bed, she clipped the paper from the fan and continued to the tiny apartment kitchen. She opened the fridge, looked inside, and reached over the leftover spaghetti and meatballs to grab the half-empty bottle of Cabernet; the eleven-dollar-and-ninety-nine cent type. Reaching into the sink full of dirty dishes, she unearthed a stout coffee cup and sniffed it.

"Gross." Sheri crinkled her nose at it and rinsed it briefly, foregoing detergent.

Drifting back into the cozy living room, she paid no attention to the cups, plates, clothing, and newspapers haphazardly strewn throughout and went straight for the couch. She'd left the TV on earlier and what had been the History Channel's "History's Mysteries" when she went to sleep was now "Ice Road Truckers."

Locked in, a devout fan, she poured the wine into the coffee cup, placed the bottle on the floor, and then turned her attention back to the show. The guys were doing the prep work on their trucks before driving over the ice road to the DeBeers Diamond Mine.

The Assistant Conductor lit a cigarette and inhaled, flicking the ashes into an unknown substance that sat on a plate next to her on the small, cluttered end table. The substance, light in color, was browning at its edges. She looked at it with the eye of a scientist gazing through a microscope at a Petri dish.

Sheri didn't sleep well at night since she'd left Matt three years ago. Though Jackie was her best friend, Sheri had never said what happened, and would never say what happened. One day they'd been living in a beautiful hilltop home in the country. The next, Sheri was dwelling in a basement apartment the size of a boxcar as though Matt had never existed.

What Jackie did know was that Matt had broken in and assaulted Sheri twice after she left him. The Conductor could never see Sheri as a victim, though. Especially since after both alleged assaults, Matt was somehow left with a black eye and split lip. Sheri's stealth at evading the subject had been polished to a high sheen over the years.

Sheri was a lot of things, chief among them a person who could keep secrets. She knew it unnerved Jackie, the wall she could construct around simple information; but after all, secrets were where their friendship had begun.

It had been after one o'clock in the morning and Sheri, who was new to passenger railroading, had just gotten back into Albany after working a late train from New York City.

As she walked up the small blacktopped hill through the dimly lit parking lot, she'd heard a weak, muffled moan.

The Assistant Conductor rushed to find where the noise was coming from, and there lay Jackie, her blond hair askew. Blood and hair mixed together to form a paste on her cheeks and nose. Her right eye was swollen shut. Sheri took thankful, immediate note that although Jackie's shirt had been half ripped off, her pants were fully intact.

Jackie noticed Sheri looking at her zipper with relief and raised her trembling hand, a tiny can in her palm.

"Pepper spray," Jackie whispered, "cures hard-ons instantly." Sheri saw Jackie's lips curling up into a smile, and looked down affectionately at her.

"I've got to get you to the hospital," she had said. "And I'm Sheri, by the way, the new Assistant Conductor."

"Jackie," the veteran Conductor had replied hoarsely from the ground. "I can't go to the hospital," she added, looking up at Sheri. "I've just got some scrapes, maybe a sprained ankle. Just help me get up."

Sheri looked down at her, conflicted.

"Look," Jackie said, becoming agitated as she rolled slightly in each direction, trying to sit up. "You can't tell anyone about this. I know you're new, but this place is horrible with the gossip; you know, telephone, telegraph, tell-a-railroader." Jackie coughed as the joke came tripping off her tongue.

"Here," Sheri finally said, though she was inclined to disagree. She placed Jackie's arm carefully around her neck and slowly raised her onto her right foot. "Let's get you home."

The Assistant carefully helped the Conductor to her car. She could see the pain in Jackie's glazed, disoriented eyes, as if she'd just fallen off a merry-go-round.

"We should go to the police," Sheri hissed angrily.

"It's O.K.," Jackie replied as she wiped the hair from her face, probing the cut on her lower lip with her tongue. "Cops got 'em already."

"And they left you here?!" Sheri yelled in disbelief.

"No," Jackie sighed. "I saw them grab him as he ran out of the parking lot--he was trying to steal a car. I got in the way."

"So press charges!" Sheri fumed. "Or go shoot his ass-- have you seen your face?!"

"I don't hurt people," Jackie replied flatly, twisting her hands together as though trying to open some invisible object.

Sheri reached over to wipe the tears from Jackie's face, but the Conductor jerked away from her, eyes cold.

"It'll dry," she said stoically.

Jackie got into her car and looked at Sheri as she started the engine. The Conductor gave a slow, single nod to her as she pulled out of the station parking lot.

Sheri considered wedging in another comment, but just stood silently, watching Jackie leave.

Jackie had never believed for one second that a "new kid on the rail block" was going to keep a secret that juicy, but as the weeks turned to months, and months to years, no one had said a word.

In Sheri, Jackie had found a friend, and vice-versa, although you couldn't find two people more different. Sheri craved adventure to the point where she perceived every situation as a mysterious, living creature full of possibility. It truly made no difference whether the conversation was about butterflies or toilet paper.

What Jackie lacked in the imagination department, she made up for in her problem-solving abilities--which were, more often than not, used to keep Sheri out of trouble.

As for their friendship, at the end of the day, they somehow always landed on the same page. Still, the railroad would always be their only common thread--and a tightly woven one at that.

Sheri loved to bring up the night their train was four hours late and at least sixty of the three hundred passengers had begun to hammer away at Jackie in the middle of the café car.

Unable to stop their screams and complaints, Jackie had closed her eyes for a long moment and then called up to the Engineer over her hand-held radio.

"Conductor on 710 to the Engineer, over." The screams subsided; they packed around her like wolves to listen.

"This is the Engineer on 710, over," he responded.

"Yeah, 710," Jackie began sternly into the mic. "I want you to bring this train to a safe stop. I have sixty passengers who want to get off--*right now*."

However, the train had been traveling at one hundred miles per hour and, as it slowed, the passengers had begun to notice the countryside, the darkness, the fact that they were in the middle of the proverbial "nowhere."

Then the screams turned to mumbling as they became more like lost pups than the ravenous wolves of moments ago.

"Where are we?..."

"This isn't a station…"

"It's dark out there…"

"I have to get to New York…"

"This train fuckin' sucks."

As the train came to a stop, Jackie opened the door and dropped the trap steps, eyes glaring beneath the rim of her conductor's hat. She walked down onto the ballast and into darkness. The vestibule was crowded with shadowy, still figures.

"Let's go, people," Jackie ordered.

And, just like that, the passenger's malevolent goals were lost to her resolve. Every person in that pack very quickly and--aside from an inaudible mumble or two--very quietly disappeared back to their seats in the coaches. Jackie climbed back onto the train, called the Engineer over the radio, and gave him the signal to go.

She walked into the café car like a pissed-off parent and -- shit-eating grin on her face -- told Sheri to keep her mouth shut, then picked up her slightly cooled coffee cup and took a sip.

Sheri would never forget that night, and anytime she'd had more than two glasses of Cabernet would throw her arms around Jackie and tell the story again and again….

Flicking her cigarette again into the substance sitting next to her, Sheri was now pretty sure it had been a small blob of ice cream from a few days before.

She finished the cup of wine and looked over at the picture of herself and Jackie on the small bookshelf across the room. Her smile dissolved like sugar in warm water as she looked at the clock. The Ice Road Truckers had long since completed their mission, and Sheri switched off the TV.

Carefully, she set the empty coffee cup on top of a stack of magazines, pushed her cigarette out into the melted blob, and went back to bed.

CHAPTER 3

Jackie awoke before the alarm was set to go off at eight o'clock and immediately thought of the pervert in the chat room. As she slipped her long, tan legs out from under the comforter, her face flushed, and she now found herself amused by what had transpired in cyberspace.

As she slid her feet into her cream-colored fleece slippers, the notice bounded back into her mind, the thought of it landing with an oppressive weight. The chaos she knew would ensue encircled her head like a swarm of gnats.

Jackie proceeded downstairs and walked through the large, immaculate living room and into the expansive kitchen--slowly this time, not as though she had done it a million times before. The Conductor stopped in front of the specialized stone hearth oven. The small, cave-shaped oven sat in the wall like a giant mouse hole.

Rebuilding the Old-World Italian stone décor had taken months and thousands of dollars to recreate and complete. Looking at it now was like having an ice pick jabbed into her eye socket.

The coffee maker sat on the far side of the green-and-black marble center island. Jackie pressed the start button, almost forgetting she had already set it to turn itself on the night before. As she crossed the kitchen and hopped up the small step into the downstairs bathroom, she noticed her socks and T-shirt in a clump on the floor.

"Sheri's not rubbing off on me," she said, quickly storming across the room, grabbing and then throwing the clothes into the hamper in the bathroom. As she started the shower, she thought of Sheri a moment, certain her assistant would know something was wrong.

She stared into the bathtub, her eyes becoming glassy. The problem was hers and hers alone. Sweeping her long, blond hair over her shoulder, she shook her head and stepped into the tub.

On the other side of town, Sheri hit the snooze button for the fifth and final time. Having apparently made her peace with the alarm clock, she went to sit up, caught her foot in the sheet, and rolled off the bed and onto the floor with a thud.

"Cripes," the Assistant Conductor giggled in a half-moan. She considered the benefits of carpeting as she lay on the bare wood floor. Finally, she sat up and looked around the room, wondering where to begin looking for her uniform in the vastness of crap around her.

Jackie pulled the white, short-sleeve dress shirt over her white T-shirt and stood buttoning it in front of the large, rectangular, antique mirror. Sitting on the edge of the oak sleigh bed, her blue dress pants still unzipped, she shook her head in disgust as she slipped her black work shoes on and stood up. The prosecution and defense were already convening in her mind.

Her conductor's hat sat on the nightstand; she picked it up and inspected it as she left the room.

Jackie and Sheri pulled up to the security gates at the Albany train station employee parking lot at the same time and, of course, the Conductor pulled in just before the Assistant, who was still trying to button her shirt as she drove.

Jackie waved through the window as she buzzed herself through security, placing the I.D. badge back around her neck as she passed through the large steel gates.

The two parked diagonally to one another, about five spaces apart as they normally did. A few cars were scattered about, with not a person in sight.

After parking, Jackie walked over to Sheri's car, waiting while the Assistant got her workbags together. Although patient, she never could understand why Sheri wasn't more organized. It seemed like an affliction of sorts.

When Jackie arrived at work, after all, she merely had to remove two neatly packed workbags from her trunk and that was it; she was ready to get on the train.

Sheri, however, was a different story entirely. Each day after she pulled into the employee parking lot, and not until, she would begin to collect her badge, radio, belt, nametag, tie, conductor's hat, ticket punch, switch keys, and brakemans lantern from various places within her car.

She'd then begin the task of trying to place everything else into her bags while simultaneously trying to find enough room, and somehow, there was never enough.

Jackie always figured Sheri was so eager to get out of the uniform, she most likely threw pieces of it off as she drove home: radio probably tossed from her belt into the backseat as she started her car; necktie pulled out from one side of her neck and off the other, then onto the floor as she lit a cigarette; I.D. tossed onto the passenger seat and switch keys thrown into the cup holder before she finally shifted gears and backed out. The possibilities were almost endless.

But within a few minutes and after what sounded like a small grunt, the two conductors were standing side by side and beginning their daily trek through the parking lot and down the small hill to sign in for their train.

"Did you get my text last night?" Sheri asked, bag rolling noisily behind her. Jackie stared straight ahead.

"Nope."

"Krans Electric has twenty off a hundred this week."

Jackie continued walking, teeth clenched. Sheri crinkled her brows as she looked at Jackie.

"Don't tell me you've run out of projects at The Castle—I don't believe it."

"Here's a project, Sher--" Jackie snipped. "Why not clean out your car?"

"Yeah, O.K.," Sheri huffed as they got closer to the door.

"Or your apartment, Sheri."

Sheri rolled her eyes and held the door open for Jackie, who walked by without looking at her.

"Or that friggin' bedroom of yours, for that matter."

Sheri chewed on her thumbnail as she followed Jackie into the building.

"Hag," the assistant grunted under her breath.

The crew area consisted of several rooms branching off one main hallway. The walls were painted a putrid yellow; the floors were made of a dreary, gray-speckled tile.

Jackie stopped in the small room just left of the entrance and began to grab her operating bulletins from the wooden shelves that sat under the glass-encased bulletin board.

Each crewmember was busily milling around. It was organized chaos: Several uniformed conductors and jeans-clad engineers bounced around between the sign-up room and the job-briefing room, going up to the station for a coffee, down to the locker rooms, outside for a smoke, or into the lunchroom. Sheri rolled her bag behind her to the far end of the hall past the employee mailboxes. Walking by the benches that ran the length of the wall, she went around the corner into the ladies' locker room.

A deep male voice came through the small metal PA box hanging on one wall and Jackie looked up.

"Jackie, are you down there? Is McKeon down there yet, anybody?"

Jackie sighed, closed her eyes, and flipped down the call button on the box.

"Yeah, Dave, what's up?"

"One thirty-eight's crew ran out of time. Outlawed somewhere a little west of Utica, ya gotta relieve 'em."

Jackie looked down at her steel-toed shoes, annoyed, and flipped the button back down.

"*West* of Utica, huh…so we're hiking, then?"

"Yep. Looks like it."

Jackie rubbed her forehead and sighed, pushing the button back down.

"Did you call the cab yet?"

"Cab's waitin' upstairs. Crew's been stuck there for hours."

"O.K., Dave. On our way."

"Roger that, Jackie. I'll have the Dispatcher let 'em know."

Jackie nodded at the PA and walked into the hall and around the corner into the locker room.

Sheri, standing in front of the sink and looking at herself in the mirror, threw a glance her way.

"We have to relieve 138's conductors," Jackie announced. "Crew outlawed around Utica, we gotta go."

Sheri, annoyed, grabbed a paper towel.

"*Around* Utica? They didn't outlaw in the station?"

"Nope," Jackie answered without emotion. "I told you not to wear those stupid shoes to work," she added, looking down disapprovingly at Sheri's black, soft-soled shoes. "The cab's waiting upstairs, we have to get moving."

"Shhhhit," Sheri slurred, "why do they call it outlaw, anyway?" The Assistant huffed as she inspected her teeth in the mirror and then glanced over at Jackie, who stood glaring, hands on her hips.

"Seriously," she complained. "Why do the feds just make the train stop wherever because we've worked twelve hours?"

"C'mon, Sherrrr," the Conductor ordered, looking down at her watch.

"It doesn't make sense." Sheri protested. "They should change that law and let us stop at the next station even if the hours of service are up. Not just, 'Hey, wherever in the woods you run out of time, too bad.' It's stupid."

Jackie grabbed the handle of her workbag.

"Get your stuff and let's go."

Sheri nodded, sighed, and grudgingly reached for the handle of her own bag.

Two engineers giggled at the women as they walked out of the crew room, bags rolling behind them.

"Nice day for a walk in the woods, girls," the fifty-somethings chided.

Jackie tried to stop Sheri, but she was already back inside.

"Hey, Joe," Sheri called.

"Yeah, Sheri." Joe grinned.

"I have something for you." She smiled as she reached into her pockets and then stopped.

"Oops, I must have left it at home. Oh wait! Here it is!" She whipped her hand out of her pocket and flipped Joe the bird and then walked back out the door.

"Shit, I should have left all of these rule books n' crap home," Sheri whined to Jackie as they approached the door leading to the station elevators.

"Leave it?" Jackie rolled her eyes. "I'm surprised you could *find it*."

"What's wrong with you today?" Sheri asked suspiciously as they entered the elevator. Jackie ignored the question and pressed the third-floor station button.

The taxi driver was waiting for them at the ticket counter.

He stood about five feet tall and four feet wide, and was covered in about a bazillion tattoos; just plain greasy looking.

"Cripes," Sheri muttered.

"Don't treat your boyfriend like that," Jackie retorted.

Tipping her head back, Sheri crinkled her nose and laughed. "You're so friggin' dead."

"Crew for Utica," Jackie said to the man.

The driver nodded without saying a word and began lumbering toward the main entrance to the station. The two conductors quietly followed him outside.

Cabs, cars, and buses lined the front of the station like a hillbilly motorcade as time-panicked passengers scurried in and out of the building.

As the conductors stuffed their workbags into the cab's trunk, Jackie leaned forward, whispering in Sheri's ear.

"I feel like we're about to be abducted by Shrek," she said uneasily, peering over the trunk at the driver, who was thumbing through a wad of ones and fives by the driver's door.

"Famous last words," Sheri giggled under her breath.

They climbed into the back seat. As Shrek squeezed his way into the front, his left ass cheek momentarily got hung up on the doorframe. As the poundage finally settled, the car made a slight moaning sound as it sunk under his weight.

"Have a salad," Sheri sneered.

Jackie elbowed her in the ribs.

"Listen," Jackie said quietly, "Wake me up when we're close."

"Wake you up?" Sheri snarled, glancing in front at the driver. "I don't think so. You're staying up and talking to me."

Jackie sighed, tipping her head back against the seat as the driver pulled out of the train station parking lot and got on the New York State Thruway heading west.

"Fine, Sher--what now?"

"I don't know," Sheri shrugged defensively. "How about your shitty attitude?"

Jackie looked over at her, brows raised, then back out the window without answering.

Shrek peeked back in the rearview at the tiff.

"O.K.," Sheri gave in reluctantly. "So what's the latest project at McKeon Castle?"

Jackie's face flushed. "There aren't anymore," she answered in a half whisper.

Sheri coiled her head back in disbelief.

"Yeah, right," she said with a quick laugh. "You haven't stopped doing projects in that house the entire ten years I've known you. If you stopped, I'da seen it on the news."

Jackie kept her eyes focused out the window. She closed them as they began to well up.

"Did you finish the…" Sheri began. But Jackie quickly cut her off.

"Listen, Sheri!" She yelled at first, and then lowered her voice. The creature in front was hanging on every word. "The house…" she began, then stopped and looked back out the window.

"What's wrong?" Sheri asked, confused.

"I can't lose it…I can't." Jackie said in denial.

"What the hell are you talking about?" Sheri asked. "What's going on?"

Jackie continued to stare out the window. "It's taken my entire life to rebuild it." She closed her eyes. "*Son of a bitch*," she whispered.

"Jackie," Sheri sat up straight. "*What* happened?"

Jackie turned and looked at her; the Conductor's gray eyes appeared black with anger.

Sheri felt a chill go through her. The look in Jackie's eyes was one she had never seen before, as though an entity of rage had just announced its residence within her.

"My house went into foreclosure."

"WHAT?!?!" Sheri yelled in disbelief.

Jackie blinked slowly. "My mortgage is paid automatically from an account I set up *just* for the house—but it was a *joint* account."

Sheri winced, and the car went quiet.

"It was my money--for the mortgage--I never thought…" she trailed off for a moment. "Remember the mistress?" Jackie asked flatly.

Sheri glanced to the side at Jackie with a smirk, "I remember *her leaving town*."

Jackie wasn't smiling. Sheri sighed. "Yeah, of course, that's why you divorced him."

"Um-hm," the Conductor agreed. "Ten months *later-- after--* I found out about it, remember?"

She looked out the window and shifted uncomfortably in her seat, sliding the radio lodged between her side and the taxi door to the back of her belt. Shrek looked back in the mirror, engrossed.

"I don't understand what that has to do with The Castle?" Sheri asked, bewildered.

"All that time, all of my checks," Jackie began, and then hesitated. "Instead of going toward the mortgage, must've been going toward trips with her, gifts for her… I guess, I mean, I don't know. I got a foreclosure notice, not the detailed asshole report."

After a moment the creature cleared his throat. "Shit, I didn't know being supported by a woman was an option! Think I'd make a good gigolo?" he asked with a snort.

Sheri immediately began laughing at the absurdity of the prospect.

"A few less tattoos and pizzas and you might be onto something there!" Sheri giggled briefly, then leaned toward Jackie.

"I *cannot* believe this, Jack," she whispered. "How much do you owe?"

"Oh, around twenty grand," she slurred, and then looked directly at Sheri.

"His friend at the bank," Jackie went on. "Real nice guy he turned out to be, too. At least now I know why I never got so much as *one* delinquency notice."

Sheri sat quietly in disgust.

"Holy shit!" The creature chortled in the front seat. "I hope he's got insurance on those *balls* of his!"

Jackie glanced at him in the mirror, taking a deep breath.

"That's without the interest, bank, and lawyers' fees--it's just the tip of the iceberg. I don't know." Her voice became a whisper. "I can't lose them again."

"You mean '*it*,'" Sheri corrected. "It's a house, Jack--*they're* gone."

"Leave it alone, Sheri," Jackie warned, then looked back out the window again.

Shrek bumbled back into the mix. "Seriously, though," he asked, "Women really do that shit? Support men 'n' all? Cause if so, I need me one a-doze!"

"Not this one," Jackie hissed, her anger covering the curves of her words thickly again.

"That's McKeon Castle," Sheri said angrily. "We'll figure this thing out." She looked out the window, torn between a sense of relief that The Castle would finally be out of the picture-- and wanting to rip Steve's balls off. "That's bullshit."

"Hey, you wit da black hair," Shrek called back, looking at Sheri.

She looked away from the window and turned her head to meet his eyes in the mirror.

"Yeah, you. Toss me a ticket," he said, looking back at her.

"Ticket?" Sheri asked, puzzled.

"A beer. There. Right there in the brown cooler."

Sheri's entire demeanor suddenly changed. She looked over at Jackie with a playful grin.

"Don't even think about it," Jackie warned, peering over at her, and not amused.

Sheri smirked as she handed the driver a beer and a five-dollar bill.

"Tippin' me kinda early, aren't cha?" Shrek asked.

"Payment," Sheri chirped. She smiled widely at him in the mirror, popping the tab on a beer for herself.

Jackie glared at Sheri as the Assistant took a long, relaxed drink.

"Ahhh," Sheri smiled, placing the beer between her legs and going for her smokes. "Hey," she said, looking at the driver and raising her beer. "When in Rome..."

"No, *Sher*," Jackie began sternly, "a little *east* of there. *Utica*. You know--where we're going to pick up the *traaiiin*."

"You really need to get laid," Sheri snipped. "If I were running the show--" she blurted, but Jackie cut her off.

"If *you* were running the show, huh?" the Conductor angrily challenged. "O.K., you've got it, Sher. From right now until we pull back into Albany, it's your show. You're in charge, *dimwit*."

"Fine," Sheri replied, pursing her lips and looking at the driver, whose squinting eyes she noticed in the mirror. She knew he was getting quite a kick out of his own mini reality show.

"C'mon *brain crust*--dazzle us," Jackie said sarcastically out of the corner of her mouth.

"It's brain *trust--oh brilliant one*." Sheri quickly retracted.

"Um, no," Jackie said flatly, "In your case it's brain *crust*."

"Driver," Sheri blurted angrily, "would you mind if I called you a *fat asshole?*"

Jackie jerked her head and glared at Sheri as if Osama Bin Laden were sitting next to her on a trans-Atlantic flight.

But the creature just laughed. "That the best you can do, sure."

Sheri whipped out her cell phone with one hand, taking a swig of her beer with the other, then set the beer between her legs and dialed. Jackie and Shrek looked on, baffled.

Sheri took a deep breath and yelled, "Thanks, Dave!" into the phone.

Jackie's expression turned to horror, her eyes bulging. Sheri had called their boss.

"Well," Sheri snapped at Dave, "We have a flat, and the fat asshole driver doesn't have a donut. Thanks a lot!"

Sheri finished her sentence as if a crime had been committed against them, but the annoyed expression quickly left her face; she took another drink and winked at Shrek.

"*Greaaaat*," Jackie said quietly, laying her head against the window with a thud.

"*OOOOOh-kay,*" Sheri replied sarcastically into the phone. "Great idea, except we're in the middle of *nowhere*!"

Sheri gave a smirk and an up-nod to Shrek, his eyes fixed on hers in the mirror, and then yelled into the phone again.

"NO! We're stuck!"

She flipped the cell shut, leaned back, and then casually took a sip of her beer.

"So, uh…" Sheri called up to the driver, as they passed the Fonda, New York exit, still about fifty miles east of Utica. "Where's the nearest pub?" She winked at Shrek in the mirror and finished the beer.

Rolling her head upright, lips pursed, Jackie looked at the roof of the cab, then at Sheri, blinking slowly several times.

"First," Jackie said matter-of-factly, "This is why *someone like you* doesn't run the show. Second, ARE YOU OUT OF YOUR FREAKIN' MIND?"

Sheri wouldn't look at her; she sat quietly staring at Shrek in the mirror.

"Oh, and driver?" she finally said, "We're in no hurry here, so pick someplace nice."

"Sheri, cut the shit!" Jackie ordered. "I'm the Conductor. I'm in charge of you, the train, and everyone on it. *That means*--at the end of the day, it's *my* ass. So get this morning mimosa fantasy out of your head. It isn't happening."

Sheri kept her focus on the driver, who tilted his head gently and looked back in curiosity to see Sheri's expression.

They locked gazes; Sheri winked at him with a slow nod, the right corner of her mouth turned up in a grin.

The driver glanced to the other side at Jackie and saw that although her head was against the glass, her eyes had shifted completely to the right, and were staring pointedly at Sheri.

"So, Sheri," the irate Conductor quizzed, "your master plan is to go drinking, then pick up the train with the *three hundred pissed off people*, then *what*?"

Sheri shrugged.

Jackie continued, "*So*, drinking in the transportation industries now… safe and acceptable, huh? And leaving the passengers stuck in the middle of nowhere…where does that fall?" The Conductor glanced at Sheri and then looked back out the window.

"Listen," Sheri said, reasoning with her, "The train's already a freak show. Its seven hours late now--*and you know it*. I mean, come on," she giggled sarcastically.

Jackie looked at her blankly, then back out the window.

The Assistant made a last effort, the driver already in her pocket. She reached down between her feet into the brown cooler. Pulling the chubby green can up beside her waist, she inched it across the seat, pressing the ice-cold beer against Jackie's blue-polyester-clad right leg. Jackie jumped.

Sheri smiled and held the beer out to her. "C'mon, it's a beer, not a keg."

"Let it go, Sher, I have enough to worry about."

Sheri nodded, stopped smiling, and looked away from her.

Jackie glanced over at her assistant, who was staring disappointedly out the window, and snapped. She jerked the beer from Sheri's hand and stared at it. The thought of losing the house was making her head pound again.

Sheri grinned, surprised, and looked over at her partner.

"What am I doing?" Jackie said, defeated. And then pulled the tab and took a long drink.

The driver was snickering so hard the car was bouncing.

"Yeah," Shrek squealed. "Let's do it. I ain't got shit to do anyway."

"One of these days, Sher," Jackie said, taking another sip, and putting her head back against the seat. "You're gonna get us fired…and I don't really need that shit right now."

"Shut up and drink your beer, hag," Sheri mumbled.

CHAPTER 4

About forty minutes or a few beers apiece later, they pulled up in front of a bar that, to Jackie, looked more like a sprawling outhouse.

THE CAT'S HAIR was written in black Magic Marker on a large, plain, wooden board hanging over the top of the front door.

Sheri jumped out of the cab and quickly went inside with Shrek, leaving her work stuff in a heap on the back seat.

Jackie got out of the cab, leaving the door open, and leaned against the trunk, arms folded. "I've got to be losing my mind," the Conductor said with a sigh.

She glanced down at her silver Timex. The bar's battered screen door screeched open a few minutes later. Shrek's sunglasses were pushed down onto the bridge of his nose; he contemplated Jackie checking her watch.

"Time's a-wastin'," the chubby creature said softly.

Jackie looked up at him blankly. She began to remove her tie, name tag, I.D., radio, and radio belt as though surrendering to the police. Placing the items methodically onto the backseat, she closed the door and looked at Shrek.

"O.K., let's go," she said, shaking her head with disapproval, and walked past him into the bar.

Although only minutes ahead of her, Sheri was already chatting up an attractive man at the far end of the bar.

As she approached, Jackie could tell by the looks of him that he didn't belong there any more than they did. He appeared to be waiting for someone but didn't seem to mind Sheri's company.

The Assistant sat next to him, playing with the small shark's tooth that hung from a black braided string around her neck. Jackie could hear that they were somehow on the subject of cholesterol, but wasn't about to ask.

As she stared down at the bar, the headache came back. Sheri continued her conversation, barely aware of Jackie's presence.

"You *law-st*, girl?" A man's Southern accent pulled Jackie back to reality. She looked up at the bartender, and knew instantly that if her father were here, he would have sworn this had to be the redneck to end all rednecks.

The man appeared lost between his forties and sixties, she couldn't tell where. His build was that of a gigantic sausage, with stubby arms and, presumably, legs. His hair was a mousy shade of pale orange, matted to his head in an unkempt fashion--from sweating the day before, most likely. His complexion was pale, with several patches of freckles that seemed to cling together in fear. Above his sunburned nose and cheeks sat brows that reminded Jackie of two thick, white caterpillars, setting off eyes that were amazingly empty, like those of a doe. Equally empty was his mouth--save for his two, front-seated bottom teeth, which looked more like something you'd avoid while eating rather than something you ate with.

"Hey," Sheri said, slapping Jackie on the back. Jackie turned and stared at her.

"We're going to a table," Sheri said, pointing to the other end of the room.

"Fine," Jackie nodded as she reached in her pocket and pulled out a twenty-dollar bill.

Shrek bumbled up next to her and pushed her hand. "Money's no good here, honey. I got-*chu*."

Her face was hard and intense. She peered over at Sheri with contempt. Jackie didn't like it… didn't like any of it.

She looked over at the Sausage. "Just an orange juice, then."

"*Yut*," the Sausage said with a single nod, and bent over to grab the orange juice container out of the cooler.

Jackie couldn't resist watching; she needed the laugh. And he didn't disappoint.

The sunburn line went completely across his back above three inches of lily-white ass crack, with a few sporadic hairs and freckles that looked like they were hanging on for dear life at the edge of the frightful cliffs.

She quickly thanked Shrek, nodded at the Sausage, grabbed the juice, and bee-lined to Sheri and the stranger.

The man was more handsome than Jackie had realized. As Sheri introduced them, their gazes locked. His eyes were captivating: translucent yet dark, with a hazy shade of gray encircling the iris, and an orange color encircling his pupils like a controlled fire. Seductive.

His gaze seemed a complete contradiction; interested, yet bored. He had very short, salt-

and-pepper hair. His skin, a sun-kissed Indian brown, had red tones that bounced off his fiery dark eyes. And although his smile was the most beautiful Jackie had ever seen, it rang false somehow.

Jackie said hello, and they shook hands briefly.

"Mark Kessick," he said with a nod. Jackie forced a half-smile and told Sheri she'd leave them to their talk.

"Hot breakfast date with the bartender?" Mark chided softly. Jackie peered back at him.

Good call for once, Sheri, she thought. Even his voice was sexy. Sensuous yet strong. Soft, yet masculine.

"Well he does look like a sausage," Jackie replied looking over at the bartender.

"Tell you what," Mark said, smiling as he stood up from the table, taking his black sunglasses off the top of his head and holding them in his right hand. He was about six-foot-one, not overly muscular, but certainly not fat; in shape. "I need to make a call, so why don't I leave you to chat and…vodka and orange juice?"

He raised his eyebrows, and pointed down at Jackie's beverage.

She looked at him and then down at her glass. "No vodka in here and this isn't what you're thinking."

The stranger smiled. "Excuse me?"

Jackie looked up at him. "This--two women, *in the morning*--having drinks at this hole-in-the-wall; we're not gonna be here long, *trust me on that*."

"Wow!" the stranger replied with a flirty smile, folding his arms across his chest. "Kinda tough on me, don'tcha think?"

"She hasn't gotten laid in a long time, Mark," Sheri said under her breath. "Doesn't do much for the disposition."

Jackie glanced at her partner. "So I'm that bad, huh?" She muttered to her.

"*Worse.*" Sheri replied, sipping her wine without looking up.

Jackie looked over at Mark, embarrassed.

He winked at her, and then walked toward the front door, putting his sunglasses on and taking a cell phone out of his jeans pocket as he went.

"*Did-you-see-his-ass*?" Sheri whispered.

"Oh, and he knows it, too. Believe me," Jackie replied, setting her glass down atop the chipped, oak-veneer table. She turned to face Sheri.

"Lookit. I went along with this thing, but we really--*really* need to get that train." Jackie stopped and looked deeper into her assistant's eyes. "Not to mention, if anyone, I mean *ANYONE* smells alcohol on either of us, we're really, seriously, screwed."

Sheri looked down at the table, disappointed.

"We'll go out when we get back, Sher, but not like this."

"O.K.," Sheri conceded. "But let's have one more, I want to talk about your house."

"Bullshit," Jackie said, glaring at her. "You wanna keep talkin' to that guy."

"Well, I wouldn't mind, but it's not the only reason," Sheri retorted defensively.

"Fine. Whatever," Jackie grumbled. She sipped the juice slowly, biding her time.

A few minutes later, Mark returned with a friend. Sheri's eyes twinkled.

"One more. *That's it*," Jackie said sternly. "I'll leave you here, Sheri. I'm not kidding, I will."

"Man, you're a hag," Sheri said as Mark and the new guy approached.

The two men stood behind the conductors talking. Jackie tried to get up from the table, but Mark was standing directly behind the chair and wouldn't step back to let her out.

Finally, she squeezed out, and they were just inches apart. She felt electricity between them.

"I'm sorry," Mark said staring down at her, still without moving. "But I don't dance in the morning. Another time?" Even being sarcastic, Mark had a gaze that was mesmerizing.

"Thanks for the tip," Jackie said, peering over at the Sausage at the bar. "I'm going for another round. I'll break the news to your *boyfriend*."

Mark's grin left his face.

Jackie, pleased with herself, walked over and asked the Sausage for another round. As she waited, Mark watched her as she studied the beer bottle labels pasted to the top of the bar.

When Jackie returned with their drinks, Sheri had glibly turned her attention to the new guy. He was also very attractive, with short, black hair, a light tan, and big baby-blue eyes. Jackie walked up to him after handing Mark his beer.

"So," Jackie asked, "do we have a name for you yet, or do we make one up?"

"Alan," he said, continuing to look at Sheri.

"Alan?" Sheri giggled. "That's it? Just Alan? Are you going to take our order now?"

Jackie started looking around the bar; her hands went up in question. "Ladies' room?" she asked. "Never mind, I think I found it," she said, abruptly walking across the room toward a door in the wall.

Sheri looked over to see Jackie peering at the black-Magic-Markered sign on the restroom door: BIKERS 'N' BITCHES. The markers' novelty had officially worn off.

"Do I even want to open the door?" Jackie asked herself aloud, looking straight ahead.

"No," Mark replied, now standing next to her. "Do you want to walk in without *knocking first*, that's the question." He grinned and winked at her.

Jackie stepped forward and opened the door.

Sheri ran over and peeked in over Jackie's shoulder. "That's disgusting." Sheri snarled.

"Nasty," Jackie said, shaking her head.

Mark walked up to them and they stepped aside. He looked into the restroom, then back at them for a moment, and without skipping a beat flushed the toilet with his foot and closed the door.

He began to nudge Jackie back toward the table, his hand on the small of her back.

"What the hell am I doing here," she mumbled under her breath.

Just then, Jackie's cell phone began to ring. Both conductors stopped.

They knew exactly who it was by the ring tone Jackie had given him. They stared at one another through the first verse.

You're a foul one, Mr. Grinch. You reallllly arrrrre an eeeeel. You're as cuddly as a cactus; you're as charming as an eel. Mr. Griiiii-inch…

Jackie took a deep breath and closed her eyes for a moment as Sheri quickly motioned to Mark and the two of them made their way back to the table.

….The three words that describe you best, and I quote, are stink, stank…

"Hello?" Jackie answered the phone, cupping her ear to avoid the bar noise.

"Yeah, Jackie? How are we makin' out?" their boss asked her anxiously.

"Pretty good, I'd say," Jackie replied, rubbing her forehead as she watched Sheri roll a quarter off her nose and into a shot glass to the cheers of Alan and Mark. "So, what's up, Dave?"

"Well, I just wanted to check in. The crew said the café is out of food and the diner is running low-- the people are getting angry."

"They're not angry about *the food*, Dave," Jackie responded sarcastically. She listened to Dave as she watched Sheri place the quarter on the bridge of her nose again.

"Just let me know when you're en route, O.K.?" he concluded.

"I will," Jackie replied into the phone and closed it.

Walking over to a window, she tried to look through the dirt and dust. The green fluorescent beer sign outside, even this early in the day, had attracted several bugs.

Staring out in a daze, she thought about the house, her parents...the money. She ran her fingers through her long, caramel-blond hair, her gray eyes glistening with the tears she was holding, and would continue to hold back.

"Welcome to our club," a sexy, soft male voice said from behind her.

"Oh, yeah?" Jackie replied, without turning around. "What club is that?" She began to swallow her deeper emotions back into herself. Her composure strengthened by the second.

"Well," Mark said, "It's certainly not every day a woman gets put in your position. I mean, it's always men."

Jackie turned sharply to face him. "What position is that?" She asked angrily. *"What-position-is-that?"*

Mark looked up at the ceiling.

"I'm sorry," he replied uncomfortably. "I didn't know it was a secret." They locked gazes. "I'm sure there's a solution," he offered. "Guys go through crazy stuff like this all the time and things work out."

Jackie turned her gaze away from his and toward Sheri. Her assistant knew, even from a distance, that she was in trouble. Jackie glared at her, and then looked at Mark.

"Thanks, Dr. Phil. I'll keep that in mind." She stormed up to the bar.

"A shot. Make it tequila," the Conductor ordered, glaring across the room at her partner.

"Atta girl!" the Sausage cheered, his two teeth tilted like cloned, yellow Leaning Towers of Pisa.

She downed the shot and winced. Squinting, she fixed her eyes pointedly on Sheri. Mark was back.

"Listen," he said, determined, "it's a stupid house. It's really not so bad."

Jackie now stared dumbfounded at Mark.

"*Stupid house*?" she asked in disbelief. "You have no idea what '*stupid house*' you're talking about." She looked up at the ceiling, and took a deep breath. "I've spent my whole life piecing that house back together--please don't talk about my *stupid* house."

She looked back down at the bar a moment as Mark looked on.

"Now I'm gonna get fired on top of it because of my '*stupid* partner.'"

"Fired?" Mark asked. "Why? What did you do? What *do* you do?"

Jackie glanced at Sheri one more time, her glare beginning to soften.

"Mark, I really have to take the reins on things here, but it was nice meeting you." She turned around to leave, but stopped briefly and turned back toward him.

"Sheri was right," Jackie added, mustering a faint smile. "You do have a great ass… .

This isn't happening either," she grumbled, walking over to Shrek. She signed the travel voucher and then walked back over to their table and pulled Sheri up by the arm.

"Sorry, Alan," the Conductor said flatly. "I'm sure she's gotten your last three addresses by now. We're leaving--*right now."*

"BYE!" Sheri called back. Jackie pushed her out the door.

"There's a taxi stand right over there," she said, pointing. "Get your shit and lets go," the Conductor ordered.

"I had to tell them something," Sheri huffed as she pulled her tie and I.D. badge out of Shrek's cab's backseat and placed them around her neck.

"Uh-huh," Jackie said as she placed her radio on her hip. "So, you ran out of things to talk about, so…

what? You decide to tell them my business? Is that how it works?"

"You were being so rude, Jackie," Sheri blurted defensively.

"Well then, why not tell them something simple and sexist like, oh I don't know, 'She's on the rag.' *That* woulda been fine." Jackie glared at her, and then threw her hands in the air. "But, no! Wait! Let's talk about the worst thing that has ever happened to me in my *life*! There's an idea!" Jackie snatched her bags from Shrek's trunk. "C'mon," she ordered.

Sheri walked over to her.

"I'm sorry," she whispered, removing her own bags from the trunk.

Jackie took a deep breath and softened her tone. "Let's just get this over with."

Within a few minutes, they were in another taxi; Jackie made a quick call.

"Dave? Jackie here. We got a new cab and we're en route to the train." She closed the cell. "Tell me you have gum," Jackie said, looking over at her assistant.

"One better," Sheri replied with a grin. "I have peanuts."

"*Peanuts*?" Jackie questioned, annoyed.

"You don't know about peanuts?" Sheri asked, surprised. "This guy I dated told me, never chew gum. Doesn't help. But peanuts suck up the alcohol so it…"

"O.K.--Just give me some."

Jackie sat quietly, looking out the cab window for the entire ten-minute trip.

"Alright, ladies, this is your stop," the driver said, parking in the woods about twenty feet from the tracks. "*I think*."

They grabbed their bags and hopped out onto the overgrown dirt road. The taxi immediately began to back its way out.

"Do I smell like booze?" Jackie asked.

"Nah," Sheri said without looking up. Jackie, picking up the workbags, looked up at her briefly, sighed, and then headed through the bushes toward the tracks.

Their ankles wobbled from balancing on the large, uneven stones, or ballast, as they followed the tracks west toward the train.

Visibility was easily a mile and there was no sign of it. If the train were within a mile, they would see the flood and/or ditch lights on the engine.

About fifteen minutes later Jackie turned around to see Sheri stopped, placing a small bottle into her sock.

"You're not at the friggin' prom," Jackie said angrily, arms folded across her chest. Sheri looked up.

"That's right," Jackie said as Sheri met her eyes, "throw it into the woods."

"We're in the woods," Sheri replied softly.

Jackie stood silent, staring at her.

Sheri reluctantly took the bottle from her sock and threw the drink toward the tree line.

They continued following the tracks west.

Finally, Jackie could see the engine.

"Peanuts," Jackie said, stretching her hand back to Sheri.

"Got it," Sheri replied, pouring a handful in Jackie's palm as if she were a nurse passing a scalpel.

The closer they walked to the train, the more anxious Jackie felt. The Conductor chewed and swallowed the peanuts and then spun around, forcefully grabbing Sheri's arm.

"Listen--" Jackie ordered, "If *one* person, just *one*, smells alcohol on us, we're fired, so I want you to keep your mouth shut, O.K.? I'll do all the talking."

"Um…" Sheri said softly, furrowing her brows, "Like they aren't going to smell it on you?"

"You're not helping. Just get on the train, and keep your mouth shut."

Jackie turned on her radio, "Relief crew to the conductor of train 138, over."

"Yeah, what's your location, Jackie?" a tired male voice answered.

"We're coming up to the engine now, over."

"Roger," he acknowledged.

The train, between the baggage car, sleepers, diner, café, and coaches, was eleven cars long.

Jackie had no idea where he was inside it.

Sheri lit a cigarette. "Take a drag," She said hurriedly.

"I don't smoke," Jackie snapped.

"I think it will help cover the smell."

Jackie looked at her, then awkwardly snatched the cigarette. Taking three or four puffs, she coughed and then let the smoke out slowly, allowing it to get on her face, hair, and uniform.

They saw a coach door open and the soon-to-be-relieved conductor put the trap stairs down, hopping out onto the ballast to meet them. He was at the rear of the train.

The two women were standing near the front, so they quickly walked back past the engine, baggage car, three sleepers, diner, café, and the four coaches to meet him.

"Hey, Jackie," Jim, the exhausted conductor greeted her.

"Hey," Jackie replied quickly. Sheri smiled and nodded. Jim was too tired to come any closer.

"Well, guys," he said, climbing back onto the first step. "Train's all yours, Jackie. We'll be in the coaches after we get our uniforms off if you need us."

"Good enough," Jackie nodded as she climbed onto the stairs behind him, Sheri in tow. Sheri poked her in the back, snickering, as they stepped onboard the train.

"*Not a word*," Jackie ordered. They closed the trap stairs and door.

CHAPTER 5

Jackie took a deep breath, pulling the radio off her hip. "Rear of 138 to the head end, over."

"Head end of 138," Pete, the Engineer, answered.

"Relief crew's onboard; we're all buttoned up, O.K. to highball to Utica."

"Roger," the Engineer replied, and the train began to roll over the rails toward the Utica station.

The smell was all too familiar as Jackie and Sheri began to walk through the coaches--a stench neither could help but analyze. Sheri crept up behind Jackie. They tried to keep centered as the train vibrated more violently as they picked up speed.

"Ass and Indian food," Sheri whispered.

"Broccoli and sweat," Jackie retorted, without turning around.

They finally made it through all four coaches and began to pass through the diner, nodding at the exhausted chef and workers.

"Hey, sista," chef Alicia cackled.

"Hey. What's going on?" she greeted and continued by.

There was no reason to fear the train attendants, least of all those who worked in the diner and café cars. Jackie knew they spent half the trip trying to hide from her the fact that they were stoned; they spent the other half trying to stay awake.

Several months ago, the Conductor had caught two of the Chicago train's coach attendants smoking pot in the baggage car and, aside from a stern "Are you that fuckin' stupid?" she had let them go.

In the months to follow, Jackie could tell that word had gotten out, and as far as trains

138 and 139 were concerned, the attendants couldn't bend over backward far enough for her.

"Sista," the chef yelled again as Jackie went toward the café.

"What's up?" she answered quickly.

"You want somethin'?" the chef asked.

"Nah," Jackie replied. "But thanks." Sheri kicked her in the calf. "Ya know what," she called back. "Late breakfast O.K.?"

"I got you, sista, you know that." Chef Alicia nodded.

Jackie turned back around. Sheri sighed with relief.

"Your breath *stinks*," Jackie whispered worriedly. "C'mon, I want to get you in a sleeper before we get to Utica."

"O.K.," Sheri replied in a half slur.

Jackie stopped and picked up the envelope that held the tickets and room assignments for the sleeper cars. She looked at it briefly and then nudged Sheri to keep moving.

They walked into the first sleeper car. It was quiet and smelled like a morning shit or two, but that was normal. On 138 and 139, the train traveled all the way from Chicago to New York City and back again. Each sleeper compartment, though closet-sized, had its own toilet that when the top was down could very well double grotesquely as some sort of table. The deluxe rooms, which were about four times the size of the roomettes, had separate bathrooms.

"Morning shit happens," Sheri said, nauseated.

They walked through the sleeper, bouncing from side to side off the hallway walls as they went.

"Train 138, clear signal CP 248, track two, over," the Engineer called to the Conductor.

"Roger," Jackie called back, "Train 138, clear signal CP 248, track two, out."

They came to an empty room, 22B, the biggest in the car. It had originally showed as OCCUPIED the entire trip from Chicago through to New York, but was penciled in as empty at Syracuse.

Jackie walked Sheri into the room, pulling the convertible couch seat out into a bed.

"Lie down," Jackie said with a sigh.

"I know," Sheri half slurred again. "But ya know you've been a real… bitch to me today, Jack. We're going to have to have a long talk about this." She ended her sentence with a soft burp.

Jackie smiled at her drunken partner affectionately.

"It's not you, Sher. When we get back to Albany we'll talk. Go to sleep. I'll bring breakfast up in a little while."

"O.K.," Sheri sighed, and sat down on the narrow, coffin-like bed. Jackie closed the door and made her way through the next two sleeper cars in the front, to the baggage car, to finish inspecting the train.

Before Sheri could lock the door, Tyrone, the sleeper car attendant, walked into the room.

"Oh, Sheri!" Tyrone clutched his chest. "You scared the shit out of me!"

Sheri laughed. "I'm sorry. Just…*just* gonna take a nap."

"Girlfriend," he said, looking at her closely. "You're not drinkin' on the job—are you?" he asked with a cartoonishly large grin.

"C'mon," Sheri replied, sheepishly. "Can't a conductor get tired?"

"*Ummm-hmmm*," the Attendant sang. "You stay here and buzz me if you need anything. This room was supposed to be occupied until New York, so it's no skin off my ass." Tyrone went to walk out the door, and turned as he began to close it.

"Lock this when I leave," he whispered protectively, and closed it the rest of the way with a click.

Sheri stood and locked the door, then lay down on the convertible bed.

She tossed and turned. Finally, she reached under her left thigh; half the bed felt hard, half cushioned. She continued to reposition around the strange lump.

"This is stupid." She quickly stood up and pulled the cushion off the metal frame and found the zipper. She unzipped the cover and a package fell down onto the floor in front of her with a thump.

In shock, Sheri took a deep breath, sat down on the bed frame and picked it up off the floor. It was a huge block of bills, about six inches thick and nine stacks deep, with a different denomination on top of each stack. Twenties, fifties, and one-hundred-dollar bills. Chewing nervously on her thumbnail, she set the plastic-wrapped stack back down on the floor in front of her. It wasn't rocket science: Sheri knew that it belonged there about as much as a mini skirt on an elephant. She stood up from the metal bed frame, checked the lock on the room door, and walked into the private bathroom. Splashing cold water on her face, she looked out at the money on the floor and grabbed a small, white towel. *The Castle*, she thought to herself, looking down at the towel in her hands.

Without another thought, she threw the pillows on top of the package, unlocked the door to the room and quickly ran to the linen closet at the end of the sleeper car. She grabbed a black laundry bag along with some sheets, pillows and towels, and then ran back into the room. She closed the door quietly and locked it.

No one had seen Jackie put her in the room and apparently Tyrone didn't know about the package, or, Sheri knew, it wouldn't have been there to begin with.

Ripping through the outer plastic wrap, she stuffed the blocks of cash into the laundry bag.

She put the bed back the way it was using the sheets, pillows and towels, creating a new cushion. Then, opening the door a crack, she threw the bag over her shoulder. Making sure no one was coming, she got out of the room, closing the door gently behind her.

Creeping hurriedly into the next sleeper, and finding an open roomette, the Assistant Conductor walked in, closed the door, and locked it.

She reached into the laundry bag and pulled out one of the stacks and began to count.

Up to ten thousand and not even scratching the surface of the one block, she heard Jackie banging on each sleeper compartment door trying to find her.

Sheri quickly stuffed the bills back into the laundry bag, tossed it onto the bunk bed above, and opened the door.

"I'm in here," Sheri called out.

"Oh, there you are," Jackie said. "You moved on me."

"Yeah," Sheri said nonchalantly. "It was too warm in there."

"O.K. Well, here's your breakfast."

Sheri stared blankly at the plate of food. Jackie studied her face.

"What's wrong?"

Sheri looked up at her, then back down at the plate.

"Nothing. That was quick, that's all."

Jackie regarded her suspiciously.

"Something's wrong—what is it?"

A voice from Jackie's hip called out, "Train 138, arriving Utica, track two on a clear signal."

"Roger," Jackie replied, squinting at Sheri. "I'll see you in a few," she said quickly and then disappeared.

Sheri decided not to count anymore until they were off the train in Albany. It was a quick assignment, one of the best a Conductor could be called in for.

Jackie was already on the trap steps as the train was coming to a stop. She climbed down, grabbed a step box, and placed it in front of the stairs. The Conductor then stepped back to let the passengers on, checking to see that the coach attendants were by their respective doors.

"Well, well, well," a sexy familiar voice said from behind her. "This has *got* to be worth something. Doesn't it?" Mark tilted his head, playfully looking at Jackie.

She turned around, her face flushed. "Mark… right?" Jackie said in a half daze. Mark chuckled.

"I'll buy the first round since you're my *conductor*," he said coyly.

"Keep it up--it's a long walk," Jackie said glancing up at him.

Mark smiled and winked at her as he walked up the stairs and disappeared into the train.

"Where's your partner in crime?" Alan appeared and asked with a grin.

"Partner in crime," Jackie repeated defensively.

"I'm sorry," Alan said, smirking as he followed Mark onto the train. "I meant to say 'the friendly one.'" He winked too and then disappeared up into the coaches.

"Shithead," Jackie said as she hopped up onto the steps and called the Engineer. "Rear of 138 to the head end, over."

"This is the head end of 138."

"O.K. to highball Utica, signal indication."

"Roger, highball Utica."

Sheri sat still in the roomette. She reached over on the seat across from her, grabbing the breakfast sausage off the plate. She rolled it back and forth between her thumb and forefinger, appetite gone.

"There's gotta be two hundred thousand dollars in that bag," she said quietly, staring pensively at the sausage. "At least two hundred."

Sheri continued to roll the sausage between her fingers, staring out the window as the slow, rocking roll became a thunderous buzz as the train sped up.

A thousand questions bombarded her mind, but it always came back to two things: Jackie's house and what kind of person would leave something like that hidden on a train?

Jackie strode through the coaches, using the headrests to brace herself as she moved up the aisles. Passing through two coaches, she was now standing in front of Mark and Alan.

"Tickets, please," Jackie said flatly.

"Beer, was that?" Mark asked sarcastically, handing her their tickets. Alan just sat there with a shit-eating grin on his face.

"Where's Sheri?" Alan quizzed again. "Don't you guys get tickets together?"

"No," Jackie said. "We have different responsibilities."

"All you do is get tickets," Alan quipped.

Jackie looked at him and nodded briefly.

"What is electrified territory, Alan?" she asked. "A Movement Permit Form-D?" Alan looked down at the floor like a spoiled kid whose orange Jell-o had been taken away. "Or how about an activation failure--"

"O.K., O.K.…. jeez," Alan retreated. "I was only kidding."

"Or we could go into basic signal rules, if you'd like."

"Shit, I was joking." Alan said, slumping down further in his seat.

"No, you weren't," Jackie said, walking away. "And no. We don't deliver peanuts either."

She could hear Mark laugh as she continued through the coach.

An older woman stopped Jackie before she reached the café.

"Excuse me, Conductor?" the woman asked. Jackie turned to face her as she sat. "What time will we be in Albany?"

"About an hour."

"Thank you."

Jackie walked into the café and asked the attendant for two coffees.

Mark tried to creep up behind her, but it's not possible; a train is one long hallway without corners.

Jackie watched him in her peripheral vision, her face growing warm as she waited for the coffees.

"Sorry," Jackie said without looking up, "no alcohol on this train."

"Yes, there is," Mark said, right next to her now. "You're just mad because you can't have any. That correct?"

His tone made her uneasy, as though official. "You're right. We're not allowed to drink on the train."

"Coffee, please. Two coffees." Mark said to the attendant, and then turned back to her.

"Where are you based out of?" he asked casually.

"Albany," Jackie replied, looking down at her watch.

"Albany, O.K." Mark nodded. "Alan would like to see your partner again. Think we should help them out?"

"O.K.," Jackie said, surprised. "We can do that."

"O.K., well, why don't you give me your number and I'll reach out to you."

Jackie looked up into his eyes; she could feel his gaze lock around hers securely.

The Conductor reached into her pocket for a pen; he held his out to her.

Jackie scribbled her number on a napkin without looking up.

"Here you go."

"Put your name on it," Mark said with a grin.

Jackie stopped and looked up at him a moment. She took the napkin back and scribbled her name.

"You know," she said with a smirk, "They say that's the *second* thing to go."

Mark gave a slow, confident chuckle.

"Maybe sometime you can tell me what that first thing is," he said with a wink and walked away.

The Conductor watched him walking away for a moment and then went in the opposite direction to check on Sheri as they slid through upstate New York.

Knowing they were closing in on Albany, she began to feel as if a noose were tightening around her neck.

Jackie stopped a few roomettes shy of where Sheri was supposed to be sleeping and sat down, resting the two coffees and her conductor's hat on the seat across from her.

She stared down at the blue, commercial-grade carpet, taking a bit of comfort in the knowledge that Steve's bank friend would be losing his job. *Even two payments a bank probably wouldn't tolerate, but how did he cover up ten?* The headache was back. She thought of Sheri and how nasty she had been to her all day. Things were just getting worse.

Looking up, she saw Mark and Alan pass the door. Jackie jumped up and peered out to see them standing in front of the big room, 22B--the one where she'd originally placed Sheri. Mark stood, hand resting loosely on his waistband, and nodded at Alan to open the door.

What the hell?

"Hey!" she yelled out; Alan spun toward her. "What's up?" Jackie asked, her eyes peering out from under the rim of her conductor's hat.

"We wanted to see what the rooms looked like," Mark answered, shaking his head *no* to Alan at the same time.

"All you had to do was ask," Jackie said, regarding both of them suspiciously. She thought of Sheri just a few rooms away.

"Well, guys, time to go back to the coaches."

"What's up front?" Alan asked. "Is it just rooms on this end of the train?"

"And a baggage car," Jackie added.

"Baggage car," Alan repeated. "Can we see it?"

She was getting a funny feeling in her gut.

"Sorry," Jackie replied. "Passengers aren't allowed in the baggage car."

Alan crumpled his brows and smiled at her.

"You mean to tell me that we wait for this train *that long*--and you won't even let us *see* the baggage car?"

"How do you know that?" Mark asked.

"Know what?" Jackie asked, perplexed.

"That passengers don't go in there."

"Because I'm the Conductor," she replied sternly.

"No, really," Mark insisted. "How do you *know* people don't go in there?"

"Well, there's an attendant in every sleeper. They know passengers aren't allowed--only the Conductor. They'd be stopped."

"But it *could* happen," Mark concluded.

"Technically, yes," Jackie answered, shrugging her shoulders. "Though I've never seen it."

"Where's Sheri?" Alan asked.

"Busy right now."

"Wait," Alan said. "Mark said you guys are based out of Albany."

"Correct," Jackie answered curtly, wanting them out of there.

"So are you guys off duty when we get there?"

"Yup."

"Well what are you doing tonight?" Alan asked. "We'll be back this way around nine. Cocktails?"

Jackie looked at Mark. "Don't know. Have your friend call me later… if he remembers what he did with my number."

Mark grinned. "I know where it is."

With that, they disappeared back into the coaches. Moments later Jackie knocked on Sheri's door.

"Hi," Sheri said, opening the door. "Sit down, we have time before Schenectady."

Jackie handed Sheri a coffee then plopped down on the seat across from her.

Sheri looked up; the red drawstring from the laundry bag dangled down, rocking back and forth like a pendulum near Jackie's head. Sheri started laughing and looked out the window as the string hit Jackie on the temple as the train rocked.

"What the hell is that?" Jackie said, looking up.

"These guys need to put the laundry in one place. How lazy can you be?" Sheri was laughing.

"Is that funny?" Jackie asked, confused. Sheri wouldn't answer, and continued to giggle as she looked out the window at the Mohawk River.

"Guess who got on the train in Utica," Jackie asked in disbelief. Sheri looked over at her. "Mark and Alan."

"What?" Sheri asked, disoriented.

"I think this Alan guy likes you."

"What did he say?"

"He asked where you were about fifteen times, and then wanted to know if we'd meet them tonight."

"When?" Sheri asked.

"Around nine. Mark will call me later, I guess. But Sheri…" Jackie trailed off.

"What?" Sheri asked, glancing up at the drawstring nervously.

The way the men were standing in front of that room gave Jackie a funny feeling. But she decided to let it go as she watched Sheri suddenly begin chewing on her left thumbnail.

Her assistant had an attention span the size of a mosquito.

"I'm going to need a little hour nap or so first."

"That's not what you were going to say."

"Let it go. It was nothing-"

Jackie's radio interrupted.

"Train 138, CP 160, clear signal, arriving Schenectady on the siding, over."

"Train 138, arriving Schenectady on the siding. Rear of coach seven at the stairs, Pete."

"Rear of seven, roger, Jackie."

"O.K., listen," she told Sheri, "Just get off here when we get to Albany. I'll meet you in the parking lot." Jackie stood and put her conductor's hat back on.

"O.K.," Sheri agreed.

As she started to leave, Jackie stopped, popping her head back in the door.

"Sher, I'm sorry for how I treated you today. I really am…"

Sheri smiled.

"I knew that since you started in on me this morning. We're good."

Jackie nodded, and then ran back through the train, quickly opening the coach door to the outside as they rolled alongside the Schenectady platform.

She leaned out the door, hanging onto the grab handle with one hand, radio mic in the other. The wind blew her hair back.

"Four cars, 138…" Jackie called over the radio, looking at the people two hundred feet away on the platform.

"Two cars, 138," she called out as the train clipped the distance in half.

"That'll be far enough when you get 'em stopped, 138."

"Far enough on 138, roger," said the Engineer, finishing the transmission with two quick toots of the horn as the train gently slowed in front of six passengers waiting to get on.

CHAPTER 6

Jackie stepped off the still-moving train with the surefootedness of a bobcat negotiating a rocky landscape.

"Excuse me," a young woman asked as Jackie placed the step box in front of the door as the train stopped. "Are we going to be on time into Penn Station?"

Jackie looked at her long and hard, arms folded across her chest.

"The train's over eight hours late. The running time is only two hours and forty minutes."

"*Ooooh-kaaay…*" the girl said indignantly, still somehow wanting another answer. Jackie took a deep, agitated breath.

"Offhand, I'd say no. Let's go folks, 138 to Penn Station. Coaches right here, sleepers in the front."

As the final passenger climbed on, Jackie stepped up onto the first trap stair, calling the Engineer on the radio.

"Rear of 138 to the head end, O.K. to highball Schenectady, signal indication."

"Highball, roger. One-thirty-eight, out," the Engineer replied.

As the train began to roll away from the platform, Jackie climbed up, closing the trap stairs. She looked out the open door and down the platform.

Two men, one older and Italian looking, the other enormous and muscular, were waving violently at the train.

"Rear of 138 to the head end," Jackie quickly called over the radio. Bring the train to a safe stop."

"One-thirty-eight stopping, roger."

The Engineer "dumped the air" so the train could stop quickly. There was a pop and hiss of the brakes taking hold and then the train suddenly jerked, then stopped moving.

Jackie's door just made the platform. She lowered the stairs once more and climbed down. Typically in a situation like this, a passenger would get a small rebuke for not being there for the train's arrival. But the older man looked absolutely enraged; the other one, wearing silver opaque sunglasses, made her skin crawl, so she thought better of it.

"This is 138, right?" the older man asked breathlessly.

"Yes. It is." Jackie replied. "If you're coming, hop on."

The large man boarded first; the older one followed and stood waiting for her at the top of the stairs.

She walked down the platform toward the rear of the train and then called the Engineer. "Rear of 138 to the head end, I'm in position for the brake test, O.K. to set your brakes."

"Roger, 138 settin' em' up," the Engineer replied.

Jackie watched the brake shoe press against the rear wheel of the last coach.

"Rear of 138 to the head end, O.K. to release the brakes."

There was a hissing noise as the brakes were releasing as Jackie watched the brake shoe separate from the wheel. She nodded and headed back up the platform.

"Rear of 138 to the head, we have a good brake test."

"Roger, 138 good on the brakes."

Jackie climbed back up the trap stairs to find the older gentleman still waiting for her. She looked at him a moment and then poked her head out the door and looked down the platform.

"Rear of 138 to the head end, let's try it again, Pete. Highball Schenectady."

"Roger, Jackie. One-thirty-eight has a highball."

Jackie closed the trap and exterior door and turned to find herself eye to eye with the older gentleman.

His eyes were black and huge; Jackie found herself extremely uncomfortable.

"Can I help you, sir?" the Conductor asked.

"Yes," the man replied, "I'd like a sleeper to New York City."

Jackie wasn't going to sell a sleeper. They were only twenty minutes away from Albany, and that would force her to breathe on everyone from this guy to the ticket agent.

"I'm sorry, sir, I think they're sold out."

"No, they're not!" the older man snarled. "The *22B* room is open in the 13810 car! The people got off in Syracuse!"

Jackie's eyes widened. "Really?" she said, realizing the man was most likely a spotter, a person to whom the company would give free tickets to spy on employees, then report back.

"O.K., sir. Well, I have no way of knowing if the room's been sold down the line. But your new crew getting on in Albany will know. You can ask them when you depart."

"I'm asking you!" the older man said, seething now.

Jackie couldn't understand the hatred in his eyes and voice.

"O.K., follow me, sir. I'll see what I can do."

Had it been a younger man, Jackie would have told him to go piss up a rope. But he was an older guy. Sort of resembled Martin Scorsese, Jackie thought to herself as she led him up through the coaches to the cafe.

The coach and sleeper ticket envelopes were sitting on the front table. She sat down and picked one up.

"You're right," Jackie said, looking down at the 13810 car envelope. "The 22B room in the 13810 car *is* open." She remembered now that 22B was the sleeper she had originally stuffed Sheri into.

"Terrific!" the man cheered. His entire disposition changed in that instant.

"What do I owe you?" he asked excitedly, ripping his wallet out from his navy blue dress-pants pocket.

"Well, it's going to be fifty-"

"Train 138, restricting, CP 143, arriving Albany, main track, over," the Engineer's voice crackled.

"One-thirty-eight, I'll spot the baggage car on the platform. Nice and easy," Jackie called over the radio.

"Baggage on the platform, nice and easy, roger," the Engineer called back.

"Listen," Jackie said to the man. "Just go to the room; the relieving conductor getting on here in Albany will take care of you after departure."

"Shewa. Shewa. Thank you, Conducta," the man said, holding out a one-hundred-dollar bill.

"No thanks. It's my job, sir," she said, standing up from the table and adding, "Just walk through the train. It's the first sleeper car you come to, walking through. First room in the front end."

"O.K.," he said, quickly pulling his cell phone out of his pocket while collecting his belongings.

Jackie ran through the sleepers, passing him on her way into the baggage car, and swung the large, steel loading door on the side of the boxcar open with a thud.

"Three cars, 138," Jackie called to the Engineer over the radio.

"Three," he repeated as the train slowed.

"A car and a half, 138," Jackie called, looking at the target spot.

"Car and a half," the Engineer responded, and slowed the train accordingly.

"Half, 138. Easy." Jackie called as the train approached the spot.

"Half," he repeated.

"138, far enough." Jackie said, as the train crawled directly on top of the target.

"138, stopping," the Engineer repeated, and the train stopped.

Jackie stepped off onto the platform through the large, square opening on the side of the car.

Jeff, the relieving conductor, was waiting.

"Hey, how's that job?" he called out sarcastically.

"*Yooou know*," Jackie said with a slow, contemptuous roll of her eyes. "No specials. There's an older man, room 22B in the 13810 car for an upgrade out of Schenectady. We were almost here so I said you'd catch up with him."

"No problem," Jeff replied casually.

Jackie rubbed her forehead. "No, wait, and you have a wheelchair for Poughkeepsie in the coaches."

"That's great," Jeff said, annoyed and shaking his head. "They never have bridge plates there."

"I know," Jackie said. "Ask the baggage department for one, and take it with you."

"Good idea," Jeff replied looking down the platform at the coach attendants.

"O.K., Jeff," Jackie said as she walked back inside the baggage car. "Train's all yours. Have a safe trip."

"Thanks, Jackie, have a good day off."

She walked back onto the train and headed through the sleepers toward the café to get her bags.

Passing the 22B room in the 13810 car, she noticed the door to the room was open. Scorsese was kneeling, the cushion ripped off the bed.

"Hey!" Jackie yelled, rushing into the room and kneeling beside him.

"Sir! Are you O.K., sir?" Jackie whipped the radio off her hip. The man reached out and grabbed her hand and the radio fell to the floor. He was holding on to it so tightly her hand was turning bright red, then white.

He sat up on his heels, pulling her down closer to him.

"Were you in here?" the man asked through an unearthly growl.

Jackie looked at him, disoriented.

"Let go of my hand, sir, I can't help you like this."

The man reluctantly released her. Jackie stood up, shaking her stinging hand several times.

"Are you O.K., sir?" she repeated, taken aback.

The man abruptly stood up and sat on the bare metal bed frame, his face nearly purple.

"Answer my question, Conducta," he demanded, staring past her into the hall of the car. "Were you in this room?"

"No," Jackie answered indignantly. "What's wrong?"

"Conducta--just tell me *who's* in charge of this room."

"If there's a problem, sir, *I'm* the Conductor; *I'm* who you speak to."

"Did I say there was a problem?" the man snapped, looking her up and down as though she were a complete moron. "Who said there was a problem?" he growled. "If you were *listenin'*-- what *I ASKED* you was *WHO* has been in this room."

"Well," Jackie answered defensively, "it showed occupied through to New York on my paperwork, but like you said, the people got off in Syracuse." She thought for a moment more. "And that's it, sir. That's why it was open."

"Now we're gettin' someplace," the man said sarcastically, throwing his hands in the air.

"Now, that's good, Conducta, except--I need to know *who else* mighta been in here."

"No one, sir." Jackie began, and then stopped. "Well, except for your sleeper car's attendant, but that's normal."

The man's eyes widened and he smiled at her. Not a friendly smile though, Jackie thought.

"My attendant…*the Attendant*," the man repeated, satisfied. He cleared his throat and stood.

"I didn't see nobody," a deep male voice said from behind her.

Jackie turned around to see the large, dark-haired man with silver opaque sunglasses standing behind her, playing with a piece of wire.

"Put that away," Scorsese ordered him sternly.

The man put the wire back into his dress coat pocket and stood blocking the door, his arms folded across his large chest.

Jackie looked down at her watch uncomfortably.

"Sir," she began. "If there's nothing else, this is my stop… and the train's going to depart soon."

"Oh yeah, shewa, shewa—" the man said, shaking his head *no* toward the man in the doorway. "Just one thing, what's my attendant's name--and where can I find 'im?"

"Umm," Jackie hesitated, trying to recall. "Tyrone." she finally said, remembering. "Your attendant for this car is Tyrone Stevens. The attendants stay in the last room of each sleeper--the ones without numbers on the doors."

The man nodded toward his friend in the doorway, who stepped aside.

"You have a good day, Conducta," the older man said, holding out two one-hundred-dollar bills. Jackie just nodded uneasily at him and hurried out of the room and ran back through the train to the café car.

The man in the silver sunglasses turned toward Scorsese.

"*Ty-roooone?*" The older man laughed. "You find that motherfucker and bring him to me. I don't care if you have to crack open fifteen heads--you bring him to me, you got it?" Scorsese ordered.

The big man nodded and left the room. Scorsese sat looking out the sleeper-car window toward the employee parking lot.

He saw Jackie walking by on the platform, and then focused suspiciously on a woman with the same uniform on carrying a black laundry bag into the lot.

He couldn't make her out.

As Jackie walked past the humming engine and across two sets of tracks, she could see Sheri turn toward the first row of cars and open her car's trunk.

"*Safe*," Jackie whispered, relieved, and walked faster to meet her.

When she got to Sheri's car, the Assistant was sitting on top of her trunk, staring at Jackie pensively.

Scorsese sat still in the room, watching the two women from a distance.

"What if the foreclosure thing is just a misunderstanding?" Sheri asked, continuing to study Jackie's face.

"I seriously doubt it," Jackie replied contemplating. "They had the dates, the amounts… I just can't believe he got them to let it go for so long."

"Steve's buddy?" Sheri asked rhetorically.

"He had to have stopped or intercepted the delinquency notices. He did *something*… there's no other logical answer."

"Still, it could be a mistake," Sheri said, searching Jackie's eyes.

"O.K.," Jackie replied, nodding her head. "Could be, but I'm not counting on it." She looked down and rolled her bag back and forth. "Everything's automated."

"Exactly," Sheri said. "Computers make mistakes, too."

"Yeah…" Jackie replied warily, "But this *many* mistakes?"

Sheri sighed and slid off the trunk. "I'll meet you at your place later, then?"

"Roger that," Jackie answered, and walked to her car. She looked down at her watch. It was 2:40; there was plenty of time to sleep.

Sheri got inside her car and started the engine. She chewed on her right thumbnail in a daze as she drove home.

Sheri threw the laundry bag over her shoulder and quickly opened the apartment door. For the first time in six months, she threw the deadbolt, then sat on the living-room floor and emptied the bag.

Jumping up and running around the corner to the kitchen, she grabbed her counterfeit pen and drew lines across a few of the hundreds.

"Yellow!" she cheered. The money was real. The question returned to her. "Who would leave this there? It's gotta be illegal, right?" she reasoned. "Or why hide it, why leave it?"

Sheri counted to forty thousand dollars, not paying attention to the easy fact that there was at least five times more left to count. She stopped and stared at the floor a moment and then separated the money into piles. One of those piles was twenty-five grand. *You're lucky I don't just let her get her hands on you, Steve-o*. She stood, walked to her landline, and dialed.

"Hi, Craig," she reluctantly greeted her attorney brother. "You working for a living yet?"

"Nope. C'mon, sis, a zebra can't change his stripes."

She felt a sick sense of relief. "I have a job for you."

"Well, I'm kinda busy right now…"

"Would fifteen thousand cash free you up?"

"Quickly, at that," Craig answered.

"Good. I need you to come over here…right now."

"The house on the hill, right?" Craig asked.

"Nope, not for a long time. Down by the river, 421 Broadway, O.K.?"

"Bye," Craig said, and hung up.

Sheri knew he would literally race over. She put twenty-five-thousand dollars in one envelope, fifteen thousand in another, shoved the rest under her bed, and then waited. Craig was pounding on the door within ten minutes.

Twenty minutes later, the meeting was over. "Done," Craig said, outside the apartment door now. "Don't sweat it. This is an easy one, trust me."

Sheri nodded and closed the door behind him. She picked up the phone and called Jackie. The line was busy.

Across town, Jackie was just hanging up with her bank.

Nice thought, though, Sher. Was worth a shot, she whispered to herself. Taking her shoes and socks off, she lay down on the couch, placing the remote on her stomach. Just as she was about to pull up the afghan, the phone rang again.

"Hello?" Jackie answered.

"Hey," Sheri said. "What are you doin'?"

"I was just getting ready to doze off," she replied, slightly annoyed. She decided not to tell Sheri about the conversation with the bank. She didn't see any point.

"O.K., so I'll see you around seven-thirty, then?" Sheri asked, even though they weren't meeting the guys until nine o'clock.

"Yeah," Jackie said, hanging up the phone and placing it next to the remote on her belly.

After thinking about it, Sheri had decided to keep an extra twelve grand out and pulled the money from underneath her bed. She took the twelve grand and placed it on top of the comforter and then grabbed five large freezer bags from the kitchen cabinet and began to separate the blocks of bills and place them into the bags.

Looking around the apartment, she finally decided to cut out a piece of sheetrock from the boiler room wall and stash the money inside, in between the studs.

Jackie does this shit all the time at The Castle--How hard can sheetrock taping be? the Assistant Conductor asked herself.

A few hours later, she had lost her patience.

"What the hell! Why can't I get this flush?"

She was covered in joint compound, a tiny blob resting on her upper right eyelash. Finally, regaining her composure, she smoothed the compound over the newly taped section of wall with the trowel, located the studs, and grabbed her large bathroom mirror and nailed it over the top of it.

She felt at ease. The money was hidden, Jackie would get to keep her house, and no one had seen her in that room. It was a good feeling.

CHAPTER 7

The man in the silver, opaque sunglasses pushed Tyrone into sleeper 22B; he fell at Scorsese's knees, out of breath. A line of blood from being pulled through the car with a piece of wire began to drip from his neck.

The man in the sunglasses closed and locked the door behind him and stood, arms folded against the door, his breathing eerily steady.

"You take my money?" Scorsese asked, seething.

Tyrone tried to catch his breath, stopped, and looked up, confused.

"Money?" he asked, frightened and bewildered. "I don't even have *my own* money," he finished, exasperated.

"Listen, you don't want me askin' again." Scorsese clenched his teeth. "You tell me *right fuckin' now* where it is. I don't have time for this *crap*."

"*Pleeease*," Tyrone groveled. "I don't know what you're talking about, I don't--*I don't*."

Scorsese looked to his friend and laughed.

"There's a surprise, ah--- lyin' motherfucker. Where'd ya find 'im?"

The man in the sunglasses stood emotionlessly.

"Baggage cah, front of the train."

"C'mon," Scorsese said, raising the frightened attendant to his feet. "Show me dis *baggage cah*."

When they got there, the man in the sunglasses pulled open the large, square loading door on the side of the car with ease. He pushed Tyrone down onto the dirty metal floor, his mouth and neck bleeding. Tyrone gasped for air, clenching his abdomen.

"Please," he garbled.

Scorsese kept a safe distance from the opening and looked angrily at Tyrone as the train thundered to one hundred and ten miles per hour. He looked at his friend and nodded.

"What's the Conductor's name!?" Scorsese yelled into Tyrone's bloodied face.

"Jackie!" Tyrone blubbered.

"Jackie WHAT?!" Scorsese demanded.

"McKeon, it's McKeon," Tyrone cried out guiltily.

The man in the sunglasses put the wire gently back into his pocket and grabbed Tyrone by his neck, sliding him closer to the opening and purposely digging his fingers into the gashes from the wire as he dragged him.

"You know what it's going to feel like when you hit the ground?" the man in the sunglasses asked in an even, emotionless tone unaffected by the vacuum created by the opening. His lips turned up in a perverse smile.

Tyrone couldn't speak, and began gasping in fright as the man in the sunglasses held his head out the huge side loading door.

"Where's my fucking money!?" Scorsese yelled. "Last chance, you no-good motherfucker."

"Jackie McKeon!" He yelled. "It has to be!"

The man in the sunglasses took a small, jagged knife with a tiny hook at the end of it out of his jacket pocket as he held Tyrone's head out the door.

He reached out and sliced Tyrone's eyeball through the lid. Tyrone screamed in shock, pain, and horror as his eyeball dangled. Scorsese shook his head.

"Now what the fuck does that do?" he chuckled.

"I wanted to see what an eggplant eyeball looked like," the man in the sunglasses replied emotionlessly, continuing to hold the screaming Tyrone out the door. He wiped his knife off underneath the dress coat and onto the back of his shirt.

"Please!!" Tyrone screamed desperately. The man in the sunglasses smiled, kneeling on Tyrone's arms.

"You like how that wire feels better?" Scorsese seethed at him.

"*NO! NOO!*" Tyrone yelled. The man in the sunglasses looked up at Scorsese.

"I don't think his ears work." Scorsese said, lighting a cigarette and casually blowing the smoke out the door.

The man in the sunglasses took the wire back out of his pocket, pulled Tyrone's head toward him, and wrapped the small wire around his ear.

"*HELLLLLP ME!!*" Tyrone screamed. The man tightened the wire, cutting through his ear. It popped off, whizzing out the door.

Scorsese looked up at the roof of the car, then down at his friend.

"O.K. Enough already, he didn't do it," Scorsese said, disgusted. He chuckled, looking at Tyrone's bloodied face and dangling eyeball.

The man in the sunglasses pulled Tyrone up to him by the gash in his neck and shook him back and forth, laughing, as the eyeball swung by the optic nerve.

"C'mon, ya sick fuck," Scorsese grimaced. "We gotta think about gettin' you some help." He laughed affectionately and tapped his friend on the shoulder.

The man in the sunglasses pulled Tyrone's arms out from underneath him, slid his battered body sideways at the opening, and then rolled him out the door.

Tyrone's limp body was immediately sucked underneath the speeding train. They felt the bump and could hear his bones crush. It sounded like pieces of hard dog food popping against the body of the train. They laughed.

"We gotta get off at the next stop," Scorsese said. The man in the sunglasses opened the door at the rear of the baggage car that lead back into the train.

"That's Croton-Harmon," the man in the sunglasses replied without expression. They left the baggage car, slamming the heavy metal door closed behind them.

Sheri picked the twelve grand up off of her bed and stared at the stack of bills uneasily. It was six o'clock. *No point in a nap now,* she thought, touching the joint compound on her eyelash.

"How the hell do I get this out of there?" she complained, continuing to gently chip at it with her fingers. She threw the money back onto her bed, dropped her clothes on the floor, and stepped into the shower.

There was a knock at the front door and the Conductor meandered over to answer it. Sheri was standing there, clutching a bottle of wine and bursting with energy.

"Hey!" Sheri greeted her. "You didn't shower yet?" she asked, disappointed.

The phone rang; Jackie yawned and pulled the bottle from Sheri's hand and skulked back into the living room to answer it.

"Jackie?" the man asked.

"This is she."

"Hi, it's Mark from today."

"Oh that's great" Jackie said, "The Alzheimer's meds are working."

"Funny," Mark replied gruffly. "We're going to be up your way at nine o'clock. We're on train 71. Where should we meet?"

Sheri stared at her impatiently.

"Caroline's." Jackie replied, looking at the clock on the wall. "They're on 71," she repeated in Sheri's direction.

"O.K. See you in a little while, then," Mark concluded.

"See you soon, Mark," Jackie said and shut the

cell phone.

Jackie headed for the kitchen, Sheri close behind.

Jackie reached into the glass-and-tile cabinets and grabbed a wine glass as Sheri took a seat on one of the oversized stools at the island. She opened the bottle of Cabernet, passed Sheri a glass, and then took a beer from the refrigerator for herself.

"I'm turning on the stereo," Sheri said, standing up.

Jackie nodded, her gaze deepening into the stone island as Sheri walked out of the room.

Barry White's voice thundered through the kitchen, bringing Jackie permanently out of her daze. "The first… The last… my everything," he crooned.

Jackie shook her head. *Sheri,* she muttered to herself. *Sheri, Sheri, Sheri…* She grabbed the beer and took a long drink, eyes closed.

Sheri returned to the kitchen, dancing her way back to the island, singing into her wine glass between sips along the way. Jackie watched her finish the drink and took another small drink of her beer.

Eyeing the black-and-silver grandfather clock in the foyer, Sheri turned to her partner.

"Get in the shower already! It's 7:30."

Jackie set her beer down and then walked upstairs to the master bathroom.

Her friend gone, Sheri quickly reached into her bra and re-positioned the stack of hundreds, fidgeting with it until it was comfortable. Then she ran around the corner into the downstairs bathroom and looked in the mirror. Aside from having gone in a matter of minutes from a B-cup to a D-cup, the top of the dress looked perfectly normal. All twelve thousand was in there. She couldn't leave it in the apartment; there was no choice.

She was frankly surprised Jackie hadn't commented on her bustiness.

The money settled into the padding folds as she began rummaging through the cabinets and fridge.

A bag of fish crackers and block of sharp cheddar were balanced between her elbow and breast as she returned to the island, picked up the goblet, and sipped the last drops of her wine.

Jackie returned twenty minutes later, turning the stereo off as she walked into the kitchen and marveled at the mess Sheri had made in such a short amount of time.

On the floor were two-and-a-half small, orange fish crackers, a burgundy-colored wine blot, and a half-eaten piece of cheese, teeth marks preserved. The counter was relatively clean, save for the two wet wineglass rings and a few crumpled napkins.

Jackie blinked slowly and took a deep breath as she picked the crackers and cheese off the floor and used one of the crumpled napkins to remove the wine rings. "Are you ready?" she asked Sheri.

"Yeah! Let's get goin'," Sheri replied, excitedly hopping off the stool.

It was a beautiful evening. The crickets sang their song as the two women walked out onto Jackie's expansive porch.

"You can always tell a female conductor," Jackie said as she adjusted the top of her low-cut black dress.

"How's that?" Sheri asked as they walked across the grass into the driveway, her short red dress and high heels as natural a fit as her long black hair.

"No pocketbooks?" Sheri asked.

"No pocketbooks," Jackie repeated with a nod.

The two women climbed into the leather seats of Sheri's 1972 black Eldorado.

"How about something a little more modern this year, Sher?" Jackie quipped.

"Nah… I love this car, you know that," Sheri replied. "Besides, unlike some people I know…" Sheri smirked, "I'm not cozy being trapped in bills."

"Yeah," Jackie replied, looking over at her and blinking twice. "You're not too big on taking care of the shit that you *do* have, either."

Sheri smiled. "Touché."

As they drove down the mountain, Sheri turned the radio on low.

"Well," Jackie commented as she watched Sheri flip through stations. "Today was pretty strange, huh?"

"Yeah, lots of strange things happened," Sheri answered quietly, adjusting the top of her dress nervously.

"Tell me about it," Jackie said, looking out the window.

Sheri, thankfully finding a good station, sang along, avoiding the subject as they wrapped down the mountain.

Arriving at Caroline's, they got out of the car and walked into the bar; it was 8:20.

The bar was dimly lit. With an all cherry-wood interior, it appeared to glow in the soft lighting. People were scattered around the room. Sheri looked over at the bar itself.

"Let's get a spot by the door, and then go freshen up," Sheri said, grabbing Jackie's arm.

"Sounds good," Jackie agreed. They sat down on two crescent-backed stools and waited for the bartender.

"What'll ya have?" The no-nonsense sixty-something greeted.

"Cabernet, and a Molson™," Sheri replied with a wide smile.

"You can go first," Jackie said, looking at her.

Sheri got up and went into the ladies' room around the corner of the bar and took a one hundred dollar bill out of her bra and stared at it.

A young woman walked in and Sheri smiled at her.

"Can you break a hundred?" Sheri asked.

"I only have a twenty." The woman answered with a frown.

"That'll work." Sheri chirped, handing the woman the one hundred dollar bill and snatching the twenty from her hand. "You can keep the rest."

"Thanks!" the woman called after her as Sheri left the restroom.

The bartender had just set their drinks down as she returned.

"So, did you hear?" Sheri asked as she handed the bartender the twenty-dollar bill.

The Conductor took a sip of her beer and looked at her assistant.

"We have to get study guides for our operating-rules tests off the Internet now," Sheri said.

"Internet… don't even mention the Internet," Jackie replied, looking down at the beer bottle on the bar. Her face began to flush.

A warm breeze flowed into the room as people came and went.

"What's wrong with the Internet?" Sheri asked.

"I don't understand the lingo, I guess." Jackie's face was almost as red as the spicy wings the woman next to them was eating.

"What happened?" Sheri asked.

"When I got the foreclosure notice, I couldn't sleep, so I went into a chat room. It was called *Tame Women*… I thought that meant normal women could go there to chat."

Sheri was already laughing. *"Annnnd?"* she teased.

"Well, I started talking to some guy and it was fine at first." Jackie took a long drink and shook her head, almost spitting it out.

"Until he asked if I was a *submissive woman*."

"Oh boy! What did you say?" Sheri was rocking back and forth, trying not to spit out her own drink.

"Well, I said yes, I am. I thought, you know, he meant will I make a man dinner, am I domestic… Until he wrote back and said: *'You won't be so smart when you're choking on my…'* Jackie looked over at Sheri, who by now was laughing so hard that her face appeared frozen, her mouth stuck open but with no sound coming out.

"Thanks a lot," Jackie said. "Needless to say, I got out of there real quick. Unreal."

Sheri nodded, but was still laughing too hard to respond. She grabbed the napkin from under her drink and wiped the tears away.

Jackie sighed and waited for Sheri to get it together; she sat quietly looking at the people around the bar. Suddenly, confused, she looked at her watch: *8:45.* Jackie looked across the bar again, perplexed.

The Conductor leaned toward Sheri, eyes transfixed to the opposite end of the room.

"What do you make of this?" Jackie nodded. Sheri looked up, following her gaze.

"I thought they were on 71?" Sheri recalled. "That won't even be in the station for another fifteen minutes though, right?"

The two conductors sat looking intently across the room at Mark and Alan, who appeared to be deep in conversation.

"Sheri," Jackie asked, puzzled, "Why did they lie to us?"

"What time did he tell you they were on 71? That's a 6:40 departure from New York though, right?" Sheri asked.

"At 7:20--he said they were *ON it...*," Jackie replied, looking deeper into her eyes.

Sheri realized they couldn't even be in Albany yet. The two women looked at each other and then down at their drinks, disenchanted.

"Let's have some fun." Sheri said, shaking it off.

"Fine," Jackie agreed. They got up from their stools.

"Let's do a count," Sheri said, as she followed Jackie to the far side of the bar. "Count how many times they lie."

Jackie nodded.

They walked up behind Mark and Alan, who spun around on their stools and greeted the women warmly.

"Hi there," Mark smiled playfully. "Thanks for coming."

Jackie smiled at him and then looked over at her partner. Sheri and Alan were staring at one another already; Jackie sighed, knowing she'd be taking a cab home.

"So how was your train ride?" Jackie asked, looking at Mark again, a twinkle in her eye.

"Oh, it was fine," Mark replied casually.

Jackie looked over at Sheri. *"That's two."*

Sheri grinned. "Did you get in on time?" she asked, looking at Alan seductively.

Alan smiled. "Yeah, no problems," he answered, taking a sip of beer.

Sheri turned back to Jackie. *"Three."*

Mark regarded the exchange. "To be honest," he began, hailing the bartender, "We never left Albany. Got a call from our boss and the trip was cancelled; we got off the train just before it departed the station."

"Oh. O.K.," Jackie replied. "Why didn't you just say so?"

"Wasn't thinking," Mark replied, trivializing.

"Decided to go out for dinner. You guys have great restaurants around here," Alan added, as he waved at the bartender.

"Yes, we do," Jackie said, contemplating him as the bartender walked over.

"Cabernet, house." Sheri chirped.

"Molson Ice," Jackie added.

Mark and Alan wiggled their beers; the bartender nodded and walked away. Sheri smirked at Jackie and then plopped down next to Mark.

Mark turned to face her. "So," he began matter-of-factly, "where did you disappear to today? You were nowhere to be found."

Sheri didn't answer at first. "On the train," she finally answered.

"On the train, huh." Mark repeated. "We watched you walk out into the parking lot. Do your laundry in Utica or something?" he asked sarcastically.

"Laundry?" Sheri replied, stiffening.

"Yeah," Mark prodded. "That's what the laundry *baaaag* was for, right?"

"Oh… actually," she replied uneasily, then smiled and leaned in closer. *"Knock-off Coaches and Vuittons."*

Mark glared at her, then set his beer down. "Knock-offs?"

"Yup," Sheri answered, pleased with herself. "Knock-offs."

Mark glanced at Sheri through the corner of his eye, and watched as she wiped a bead of sweat from her forehead.

"Hmm. I thought maybe you won the lottery or something," he quipped. "You O.K.?" he asked suspiciously as Sheri began to fidget with the top of her dress again as though there were ants in it.

"Yeah. Oh, yeah, I'm good. Gonna go for a smoke." Sheri quickly got up from the stool.

Alan called over to Mark, "Scared her away already, huh?"

"Must be my cologne," he sighed, studying Jackie's expression.

"Boy, your friend has a pretty serious habit there," Mark said glancing toward the door, and then looked directly at Jackie.

"Nah," Jackie retorted. "She's just bound and determined to keep that Philip Morris stock on the charts."

Mark smiled, but his gaze remained steady. "Knock-offs, huh?" he probed.

"Knock-off what? I'm lost." Jackie sipped her beer.

He looked down at the bar, then over at Alan. "Sheri's interesting."

Alan quickly looked over Jackie's shoulder at Mark.

"Yeah?" he asked, disappointed.

"Yup," Mark replied without emotion, and took a long drink of his beer.

Jackie watched the exchange, confused.

Alan looked at Mark and nodded toward Jackie behind her back.

"Possibly," Mark shrugged, and then looked at her.

"You fish?"

"I love to fish," Jackie replied casually as she sipped her beer. "Only in the ocean, though. I like to keep what I catch." Jackie set her drink down.

The two men looked at one another and laughed.

"No catch and release?" Mark asked.

"Nah, what's the point?" Jackie replied, looking toward the door for Sheri.

"Just do it for the sport," Mark said, his piercing eyes regarding her closely. "*Catch a big one--and win a prize...*"

"Like I said, I'm not into catch and release." Jackie drank the rest of her beer and looked toward the door again.

"She'll be better when she gets back," Mark said flatly.

"She'll be better? What's wrong with her?" the Conductor asked defensively.

"I think she was a little *warm*," Mark answered sarcastically with a skyward glance.

"Warm? It's thirty degrees in here!" Jackie replied in disbelief.

"I know," Mark said with a nod, as he sipped his beer. "Then *you* tell *me*."

Jackie looked at him a moment, and then stood up and walked outside the bar to find her friend chain-smoking. Three butts had already accumulated at her feet.

"Holy shit! Who pulled the string out of your back?" Jackie asked, looking down at the ground. "You could use the butt can, at least, Sher," she snipped, "I mean, it's *right there*."

The two men came outside.

"Everything all right, ladies?" Mark asked.

"C'mon," Jackie said to her assistant. "Come back inside."

Sheri took a long last drag, looking at Jackie as she blew the smoke out, then dropped the cigarette on the ground next to the butt can. Jackie slapped her on the arm.

Alan walked back inside first, Sheri following close behind him.

"Piece of gum?" Mark asked softly from behind Jackie. His voice made her knees weak.

"Sure," she replied, turning around to face him.

"It's an interesting job you have," Mark said, handing her a piece of sugar-free peppermint.

"It's different," Jackie replied, shrugging her shoulders.

Mark looked down at the butt holder. He smiled as he looked at the four butts on the ground next to it, and took the can's top off. He laughed as he threw the gum wrapper inside.

"Well, that's nothing," he chuckled, looking into the can and seeing the cash.

"Huh?" Jackie asked, confused.

Mark quickly put the top back on. "Let's go inside. I think its Dolly Parton's round," he said with a grin.

They sat on the stools, side by side; Mark looked over at Sheri.

"It's your round," he said glaring at her.

Sheri looked at Jackie uncomfortably. "I don't have any money on me."

Mark laughed. "That's true," he said, and looked over at Alan.

"No problem," Jackie replied unfazed, and put a twenty next to her glass on the bar.

"Nice friend you have there," Mark intoned to Jackie. "You guys tell each other everything?"

"Pretty much," Jackie nodded.

"Pretty much," he repeated, contemplating Sheri. He leaned toward Jackie.

"We have to get going here, but I'd like to see you again."

"I think I'd like to see you again, too," she replied softly.

He motioned to Alan that it was time to go. Alan and Sheri said their goodbyes as he got up from the stool.

Mark leaned down and whispered in Jackie's ear.

"You have a pretty nice ass yourself, by the way."

She smiled at him; her face flushed. Mark winked at her, and then headed for the door.

Jackie looked down at the bar a moment then turned her attention back to the two men.

"Mark," she called out as they were about to leave.

"Where did you guys have dinner?"

He stopped, slowly turned back around and looked at her blankly. *No answer.*

"C'mon… the restaurant? The street? Something..." Jackie looked at him pointedly.

He gazed at her for a long moment, looked up at the ceiling and sighed, then slapped Alan on the shoulder. He followed Alan out the door without turning back.

"We're not gonna see them again," Jackie said, raising her eyebrows briefly.

"Why not?" Sheri asked, bewildered.

"They're married, Sherrrr."

"How'd you get that?" Sheri asked, crinkling her nose at her.

"They even lied about going to dinner," Jackie said, disgusted. "That's friggin' pathological."

Sheri began to fidget with the top of her dress again. "That Mark guy was acting strange, anyway. C'mon, let's go to The Castle, get a pizza or something."

"O.K.," Jackie replied, disappointed.

They walked out of the bar and Sheri stopped, looking down at the butt can. Jackie continued walking toward the parking lot. She took the top off of the large metal can and looked inside.

She lit a cigarette, using a whole pack of matches at once, and then threw the flaming matchbox into the butt holder. The flames shot up the sides as she ran to catch up with Jackie.

CHAPTER 8

They drove to Mick's Pizza in silence. As they wound their way back up the side of the mountain, the Conductor's cell phone rang. Jackie was holding the eight-cut, pepperoni-and-mushroom pie on her lap, but reached under the pizza and retrieved the cell from her garter. She looked at the number.

"Restricted," Jackie noted, looking down at it. "Probably the dispatcher."

"I'm not working tomorrow," the Assistant Conductor huffed.

"Me neither," Jackie replied as she reluctantly answered it. "Hello?"

"It's not whatever you're thinking," a calm male voice said.

"I don't care what it is, Mark. I've been lied to enough to fill the Hudson with it."

"It's not about morals," Mark countered.

"For the guy, it never is," Jackie quipped.

"No, *this,* Jackie. *This*, tonight… I'm not married, if that's where you're going with this."

"I don't give a shit, Mark." She found herself more disgusted as she spoke.

"Listen to me," he said calmly. "You may be in danger. You *and your friend.*"

"You're an idiot," she said sharply. "Next time, go for a stewardess." With that, she slapped the phone shut. Thirty seconds later, it rang again. Sheri threw her hands in the air, and then grabbed the wheel again.

"Just be nice to him, Jackie. Men do stupid shit sometimes. So what?"

The phone continued to ring. As they came around the final stretch back to her house, Jackie picked it up.

"Mark… Oh, hi Jeff," she said, surprised. Her gray eyes widened as she listened, looking over at her friend. "Are you kidding me?" she responded, upset. "What? What!" Jackie yelled in disbelief. "Well, how?" she asked. "That doesn't make sense…."

Sheri could see it was bad news.

"Wow," the Conductor whispered. "O.K., thanks for calling, Jeff." She gently closed the phone.

"You'll never believe this," Jackie said somberly as Sheri pulled into her driveway.

The Assistant sat quietly, hands clenched around the steering wheel.

"You know Tyrone Stevens?" Jackie continued.

"No," Sheri answered, looking out the window.

"*Tyrone*, Sher. Didn't you see him today? He was the attendant in your sleeper."

"Oh, O.K." Sheri replied, keeping her gaze out the window. "I know who you're talking about."

"He's *dead*," Jackie whispered.

"Dead?" Sheri quickly looked over at Jackie, eyes wide.

"Jeff said he fell out of the baggage car. He must've been smoking out the side door or somethin'."

"That doesn't sound right," Sheri replied uneasily.

"No, it doesn't. But that's what they think happened."

"You can't fall out the baggage-car door," Sheri insisted. "I mean, no one would stand that close to it; the opening is huge, it'll suck ya right out."

"Well, they're waiting on a toxicology report. They figure he was on something." Jackie frowned. "And…"

"What?" Sheri asked, searching Jackie's face worriedly.

Jackie closed her eyes, "They had to use sandwich bags to collect the pieces that were left of him."

As they came to a slow stop in front of the garage, they sat in silence, looking at one another.

"He was fine," Sheri murmured, beginning to tremble.

"I know," Jackie said, as Sheri removed the keys from the ignition.

"C'mon, let's go inside, this is really freaking me out."

They got out of the car and walked slowly across the grass up onto Jackie's front porch, then opened the door and stepped into the foyer and slipped off their heels.

"There's no way that could happen," Sheri insisted, as she headed for the bathroom.

"Wanna glass of wine?" Jackie asked somberly.

"Nah, I'm good." Sheri called back, and closed the bathroom door behind her.

She took a deep breath, and sat down on the side of the tub, staring at the checkered bathroom mat. *How could that happen?* She chewed her fingernails anxiously, thinking about the money stashed in the sleeper car. *It was an accident,* the Assistant Conductor reassured herself nervously.

She stood up from the tub, splashed her face with cold water, and looked at herself in the mirror. *Coincidence.*

Jackie, now in the kitchen, had poured her a glass of Cabernet anyway, and Sheri grabbed it, drinking it down quickly. The Conductor stared at her, brows raised, taking a tiny sip of a soda and setting it down.

"What's your deal, Sher?"

"Nothing. I'm good," Sheri replied without making eye contact.

"O.K., well, you can save that bullshit for someone who doesn't know you," Jackie said, staring at her partner. "C'mon," she added, grabbing the pizza, napkins, a container of parm, and her soda. "I'm tired. Let's go in the living room and listen to some music."

"O.K.," Sheri said, quickly refilling the wine glass and following her to the living room.

The two sat curled up eating pizza on opposite ends of the couch. They stared into the chronically unused fireplace and made small talk.

Eventually, Jackie fell asleep; Sheri sat thinking nervously about the money in the boiler room…and Tyrone. She glanced around the room as she sat there sipping her wine. *She put so much into this,* Sheri whispered, looking at her friend, concerned, as she slept. The fireplace began to give her the creeps and she turned her gaze away from it.

Sheri set the glass down and put her head on the arm of the couch.

This house is a prison, she whispered as she finally drifted off.

They were awoken the next morning by the ringing of Jackie's phone.

"What the hell?" Jackie asked, disoriented, as she fumbled around on the plush, hunter-green area rug for her phone.

"Hello?" she said into the phone after a moment. "What?" she asked breathlessly, sitting bolt upright. The small afghan she'd draped over herself dropped to the floor. "Are you serious?! Really?! This is unbelievable!" Jackie yelled into the phone.

Sheri sat quietly, knowing it was Craig. She pulled the tiny blanket up, concealing her grin.

"Holy shit! Thank you! Thanks… no, it's O.K.——really." The homeowner snapped the phone shut, and threw it across the room, aiming for a chair. It slid across the hardwood floor with a hiss as she circled around the room with relief.

"What is it, Jack? What's going on?" Sheri asked, trying to sound surprised.

"It was the bank's fault. The *BANK'S* fault!" Jackie said relieved. "*He never touched the money*! The bank was putting it under the wrong account! That was the manager calling to personally apologize. The *Castle*--is safe!" she cheered as she glided around the room.

In that instant, Sheri knew she had done the right thing.

"Let's go out to breakfast," said the owner of McKeon Castle, excitedly leaping two stairs at a time up to her bedroom.

"Fine, but I need something to wear," Sheri called after her.

"Well, come up and pick something out then!" Jackie yelled back.

As Sheri entered the bedroom, she was greeted by a flying ball of socks to the side of the face. She laughed.

The two conductors put on sweats and bounded onto the front porch.

They stopped suddenly, looking in front of them, focus glued onto the black Hummer parked sideways on the grass directly in front of the porch steps.

The driver, wearing silver opaque sunglasses, walked around to the other side of the vehicle. And without so much as acknowledging the women, he opened the back passenger door.

As the older man stepped out onto the grass, Jackie realized she had met him somewhere before.

"Hello, ladies," the man said warmly as he approached the porch. He extended his right hand toward the homeowner.

"You're Jackie McKeon, is that right?"

"Yes, I am."

"O.K., good. Now we're gettin' someplace." The stranger's eyes seemed to darken. "I was on your train yesterday and lost somethin'. I hear you know where it is."

The warm liquid trickled between Sheri's thighs; she found herself grateful for having chosen Jackie's black sweat pants, just by pure dumb luck.

Jackie's eyes widened in acknowledgment.

"I know you now!" She smiled. "Scorsese! You got on at Schenectady, right?"

"*Scorsese?*"

"Oh, just noticed a resemblance." Jackie said, then became uneasy.

"*Thanks*," the elder Italian chuckled.

She regarded him for a moment.

"Sir, how did you end up here? I mean, there's a Lost and Found in every station. You must have gone through a lot of trouble to find me."

"No trouble, believe me. In fact," Scorsese said, taking a step closer, "You'd be surprised *just how easy it was* to find you."

Sheri tried to pull the urine-logged sweats away from her leg.

"O.K., well I didn't find anything, and none of the attendants reported anything to me." She turned to her left. "Anyone say anything to you?" she asked Sheri.

"No, not that I can remember. Hi," Sheri said to the man with an uneasy grin.

"Who was working the sleeper you were in?" Jackie stopped herself short. "The attendant had a bad accident..."

Scorsese didn't seem to be listening; he turned his full attention to the Assistant. His large, black eyes swallowed Sheri whole.

"I'm sorry; I didn't catch your name," the man said, now standing directly in front of her.

"Cindy." Sheri glanced at Jackie uneasily. "Cindy Jones."

As the Conductor watched the exchange, disappointment enveloped her.

"Nice to meet you, Ms. Jones." His eyes never moved from her.

Just then a navy-blue Blazer with all the windows blacked out stopped just outside the driveway. Scorsese turned and looked at it, then nodded toward the tinted window of his own vehicle.

The driver, who had returned to the Hummer, stepped back outside and walked toward them. The Blazer just sat idling in the road.

"Nice house," Scorsese said, agitated, as the driver escorted him back to the vehicle.

The Blazer sped out even before Scorsese was back inside.

"Fuckin' rat bastards, *what*, they think I didn't see 'em?" he said under his breath.

The door shut, and the Hummer slowly left the property.

"*What-the-hell* was *that* all about?" Jackie asked angrily.

"I don't know, Jackie, but I have to use your bathroom, so unlock the door, please," Sheri replied uncomfortably.

Jackie bit her lip as she unlocked the deadbolt.

"What did he leave, *Sherrr*?" the Conductor demanded as Sheri ran up the stairs.

Jackie stood fuming, arms folded, at the bottom of the staircase. Sheri pulled up a new pair of pink sweats and walked back down.

"A little cash," Sheri finally replied, annoyed.

"A *little*?" Jackie yelled. "A *little* doesn't make you hunt down the Conductor in a seventy-thousand-dollar vehicle!"

"Gimme a break," Sheri answered, agitated, as she reached the bottom of the staircase. "It was like three grand."

"YOU TOOK THE GUY'S MONEY?!" Jackie yelled in disbelief.

"It wasn't like that at all, so don't accuse me. It was hidden in a cushion."

"Three grand, huh?" the Conductor said, putting her hands on her hips.

"*Yup, three*."

Jackie rubbed her forehead. "Let's just go to breakfast--you're buying," she concluded sarcastically.

"Actually, you have to," Sheri said, remembering the butt can.

The Conductor nodded. "That figures."

Sheri sat quietly looking out the window as they descended back down the mountain. She could still see Scorsese's black eyes looking into her, evaluating her, dissecting her.

But her friend's house was safe, and that was all that mattered. She contemplated getting the rest of the money and throwing it in the neighbors' garbage or something.

"You know," Jackie said, breaking the silence, "I never knew you to steal."

"And you still don't. It was hidden, Jackie, left behind. What would you have done?" Sheri snipped defensively.

"I would have given it to Lost and Found," Jackie snapped back at her.

"Bullshit. You know as well as I do that no one would have claimed it." Sheri retracted.

"Guess again, brain *crust*," the Conductor replied tersely.

"No, I mean, one of the ticket agents would have stuck it in their pockets, and that woulda been the end of it."

"Then that's their problem. Listen, I don't want to argue, Sher, but you have to do things a certain way out there, or you get problems, anyway you want to look at it."

"You mean if you found a bunch of money hidden on your train, you wouldn't take it?" Sheri chuckled.

"That's exactly what I mean," Jackie said, looking into her eyes.

"Yeah, but what if it were enough to pay for, like, your house; I mean, if it were a real issue… even then?"

"Especially then."

"O.K. But, what if it was a lot of money, not like three thousand, but something crazy like *three hundred thousand*, then what?"

"Then I'd take off and start a treasure-hunting business off the Keys," Jackie laughed sarcastically.

"Treasure hunting sounds like a good time," Sheri whispered.

"So does paying my mortgage."

The Assistant Conductor looked out the window.

"Yeah, you've been paying for that your entire life," she complained. "What would it take to get you out of that damn house?"

"A lot more than three thousand dollars," Jackie replied flatly.

The two women sat silently at the diner table as the forty-something waitress grudgingly placed the ham and eggs in front of them, as though they were personally responsible for her missing her calling--pole dancer or bar maid, Jackie couldn't be sure.

Jackie sat staring at Sheri and then pushed the plate away. Sheri folded her arms defensively.

"How could you steal from someone like that?" Jackie asked, shaking her head, disgusted.

Sheri stood up from the table.

"You don't believe me, I'm not doing this. Take me back to my car."

Neither of them noticed the Hummer pull up outside as Jackie nodded; teeth clenched, and stood up from the table. By the time they were back inside Jackie's car, the vehicle had disappeared.

They drove back through the mountains in silence.

Jackie parked in the driveway and got out; Sheri walked to her car.

Jackie stood on the porch flipping through her keys tensely. "You have to have some stability in your life, ya know," she told Sheri without looking up. "Not everything is a big joke."

Sheri nodded as she opened the car door. "Well, there should be more to life than bills and bad memories," she countered.

"Maybe, I don't know anymore," Jackie replied softly.

Sheri nodded, got into the Eldorado, and pulled out of the gravel driveway. At the bottom of the mountain, slowing as she approached her street, the Assistant Conductor thought she caught the black Hummer in her peripheral vision. She quickly looked to her right into the liquor store parking lot. *Lincoln Navigator. Phew.*

Seeing the two-for-one special sign in the window, Sheri pulled in and grabbed two bottles of Cabernet. She stuffed the two bottles into her workbag in the trunk, got back in her car, and drove the rest of the way home.

The Assistant Conductor never noticed the navy-blue Blazer parked across the street from her small apartment. She pulled into the driveway and then quickly went inside, forgetting the wine in her workbag.

She walked into the boiler room, turned the light on, and examined the wall and mirror. She left the room, then returned and did it a second, then a third time.

The consequences of what she had done had begun to introduce themselves. She lay down on the couch on top of the socks, shirts, papers, and pillows and stared up at the ceiling nervously. She couldn't get Scorsese's dark, sinister eyes out of her mind. As she rolled over and sat up, a small pink ankle sock, fabric softener sheet still attached, fell onto her right foot.

They're coming for you. The words whispered through her mind and the headache started. She put her face in her hands and rocked back and forth. The voice was certain, matter-of-fact, and cold. *They're coming for you.*

Sheri stood up and returned to the boiler room, opening the door; her fear and stress were palpable now. She wiped the sweat from her brow and switched the light on, then off again, over and over, staring at the mirror.

Finally, she went back into the living room, picked up the phone, and called her friend.

"Hello?"

"Hey," Sheri cackled. She wanted to tell her everything.

"What's up?" Jackie asked with a yawn.

Sheri stopped herself short, realizing Jackie would give up the house before doing anything dishonest.

"Just wanted to say hi," Sheri managed a chuckle.

"O.K.," Jackie laughed, and hung up the phone.

Returning to the boiler room, Sheri blinked several times, staring at the mirror against the newly taped wall. She switched the light on, then off again.

Paranoid, she crept out of the boiler room and peered out from the peep hole in the front door. There was no one there. She checked the deadbolt. It was set.

You're losing it, Sher. Get it together, she whispered uneasily to herself, the stress making a buzzing sound in her head. The pain and pressure she felt in her right temple was almost unbearable.

I've gotta get rid of this money, she said to herself as she slipped a soft, blue-flannel shirt over her head and lay down atop her plain white goose down.

Finally, the buzzing stopped, the headache subsided, and she fell asleep; it was three o'clock in the afternoon.

CHAPTER 9

Jackie poured herself another cup of coffee and walked through the foyer to the living room. Blinded by morning light, she never noticed Mark standing in the doorway, watching her.

He knocked three times gently on the frame and she spun around, startled, coffee spilling onto her white silk tank top and boy shorts. She stood frightened, looking at him through the door's heavy glass pane.

"What's up?" she asked, her tone defensive, keeping a safe distance between herself and the door.

"Lookit," he began with authority, "You and I are going to talk sooner or later--you can bank on it, so let's do it now."

"Are you a stalker?" Jackie asked, frightened.

"Jackie," Mark began, shaking his head. "You don't know the half of it."

"Please, I don't know how you found me…"

He cut her off. "You're not listening. Just open the door please."

"Leave me alone!" Jackie yelled, looking frantically around the room. "I'm calling the cops!"

She ran to the coffee table, picked up her cell phone, and spun back around. "And who the hell are…" but he was gone.

She stepped barefoot onto the front porch and looked in both directions, then down the driveway. Not a vehicle in sight, and not a sound. She shuddered and quickly went back inside, closing and locking the door behind her.

She dialed Sheri's number angrily.

"Hello?" Sheri answered in a daze, looking at the time. It was morning; she had tossed and turned nearly around the clock.

"Mark just showed up here, Sher! He really scared me!"

"What? Are you O.K.?" Sheri asked nervously.

"Yeah, but… lookit, we have to talk, right now. I'm coming over."

"I can't, Jack. I'm…"

"What? *You're--what*?" Jackie was livid, yelling into the phone.

"I'm coming over--and *you* better be there!"

Sheri looked at the phone as Jackie hung up.

"Eight o'clock in the morning and you '*have to talk*', huh?" Sheri huffed, throwing the phone onto the couch and sliding a pair of pale Levi's up over her slender thighs.

Half an hour later, she heard knocking at the front door and set her round red brush back on the sink ledge. It was a purposeful knock, and she knew, walking through her small bedroom to the front door of her basement apartment, which led into the driveway, that it had to be Jackie.

"Open-the-door," the Conductor ordered. Sheri grappled for the deadbolt and pulled the door open. Jackie stormed inside, peering around as if she were a drill instructor doing a spot check for a speck of dust.

"What's going on here?!" Jackie yelled.

"I dunno."

"No, you *do* know!" Jackie glared at her. "Yesterday, that guy showing up at my door, and Mark today! Cut me some slack, I'm not stupid!"

"*I-don't-know.*" Sheri skulked out of the doorway through to the kitchen, Jackie on her heels.

She hurriedly whipped the refrigerator door open, grabbing the half-empty bottle of Cabernet. Jackie snatched it from her as she turned around.

"What the hell are you doing, Sher? What's the matter with you? It's eight-thirty in the morning!"

Sheri stared down at the floor, the right side of her head pulsing.

"I told you it was three thousand dollars!"

"O.K. Well, then, why is Mark showing up at my door now? He's obviously working for Scorsese, or how the hell does he know where I live?"

"Huh?"

"How does Mark know where I live? Sher, cut the crap. What happened in that room?"

"I *toooold* you--I found money in the cushion."

"Is that all you found? Sure you didn't find Hoffa or something while you were at it?"

"Oh, screw you, I told you I found money."

"Well, give it back!" Jackie yelled.

"Why?" Sheri asked. "What good will that do now?"

"Why? Because I'm getting stalked, that's why. And you'd know that if you could stop thinking about yourself for one second."

"*Myself?* Myself? You know what? You don't even know. You are the biggest prude—bitch--I've ever met," Sheri replied defensively.

"That's how you feel, huh?" Jackie's eyes were pointed, cold.

"Yeah, it is," Sheri answered quietly.

Jackie walked back through the apartment toward the door.

"Just make sure you're on time to work. I don't feel like hearing another one of your excuses today. Think you can handle that?"

"Don't worry about me, Jackie… it's not your strong suit."

Jackie turned back briefly and nodded, teeth clenched. Sheri slammed the door behind her and walked around the corner to the boiler room again.

Sheri lay down and curled into a ball in the corner. It had been quiet a long time before she left the room. She pressed her head against the door, her temples pounding.

Finally, lifting herself up, she re-entered her apartment and, peering out into the empty living room to check the clock on the wall, suddenly jumped up frantically, looking for her uniform.

"Jackie's gonna kill me."

Throwing on the white dress shirt and grabbing her car keys, she flew out the door into the driveway, sockless, and climbed into the car.

Her hands shook as she fumbled in the consol for the lighter. *Get it together. Get it together.* Her hands finally stopped shaking. Taking a deep breath and closing her eyes, Sheri lit a cigarette.

She didn't feel well. Her face was pale and pasty and the cold sweat seemed to laminate her into what looked like a fearful mannequin.

A few minutes later, buzzing herself through the security gates at the train station's employee parking lot, she quickly parked diagonally and then fumbled around the car trying to get her work gear together.

The locomotive roared on the main track as though reminding her she was out of time.

Screw it. She slammed the trunk shut and jogged to the train, her bag flipping as she ran. She dragged it sideways by the handle up the platform.

Jackie's conductor's hat sat evenly across her brow, her gray eyes sharp-shooting daggers as she watched Sheri running toward her at the rear of the train. The assistant jumped onboard, avoiding eye contact as Jackie continued to direct the passengers.

Quickly turning her radio onto the proper channel and smoothing her bangs under her hat, Sheri jumped back out onto the platform.

"Why are you lying to me?" the Conductor asked, continuing to monitor the passengers getting on at her door.

Neither of them noticed Mark as he blended with the passengers boarding toward the front of the train.

"I didn't lie. I told you I found money in that room."

The Conductor turned her head toward the Assistant.

"O.K., fine. Go up three cars and start getting tickets. I'll meet you in the middle. Then, *we're going to talk.*"

"O.K.," Sheri agreed, and began to walk away.

"One thing, though," Jackie said, and her assistant turned back and looked at her.

"We're in trouble here, so think real hard about whether you stole anything else."

Sheri walked away, frustrated, and got on the train a few coaches up. She could hear Jackie call the Engineer to depart the station. Wobbling, she tried to keep her balance as the train picked up speed. She walked to the front of the train to start collecting tickets.

The head coach was locked and not in use, for whatever Jackie's reason. The Assistant Conductor peered through the door and could see there was a *dead head* in there. Dead heads were employees only working in one direction.

Sheri took out her long coach key, opened the door, and meandered up to see who it was. She was sure to lock the door behind her, as all passengers are cursed with "the other coach is always greener" syndrome.

"Oh, hi, Ken," she said, now wishing she hadn't come up.

"Hey. You hear about Tyrone, the sleeper attendant?" her coworker asked excitedly, without wasting time.

Ken was the most useless, nasty conductor the railroad had to offer. Fifty-nine years old and poor. Rail legend had it that all of his money had gone to beer and strippers in Chicago. Now, reduced to a rumor monger.

"Yeah, I heard."

"Well, you know damn well he didn't fall out that door." Eyes gleaming, in his glory; a juicy rumor in the making, after all. "He probably messed with one of those girls. I told those crews many times--*Never mess with any girls traveling together in those sleepers.*"

"Do you mean lesbians?" she asked mockingly, unable to contain her contempt for him.

"Strippers," he whispered, even though the car was empty. "*The strippers.*"

She laughed at him condescendingly.

"Oh, so two evil strippers pushed a man to his death. You're losing it, Ken."

He became angry. "No, Miss Know-It-All. The Chicago Family prob'ly got 'em!"

"Family?"

"The Mafia, mob...*you* know. Ever see 'Goodfellas'? Sheesh, when the hell were you born?"

Sheri's face began to itch. She scratched her right cheek; the buzz had begun to return, but she was determined to stay in control. It was only Ken, after all—-no-good loser who'd talk shit about his own mother as easily as he sipped a first beer.

"O.K.," she said, forgetting about collecting the tickets. She plopped down opposite him on the front four-seater and put her feet up, resting her conductor's hat on her lap.

"So, the mob's protecting strippers? That doesn't sound very lucrative."

"No, protecting their money," he hissed.

Her stomach became queasy. She could feel her mouth start to go dry.

"What?" she asked softly.

"Hey, your face is white. You O.K.?"

"Yeah-yeah. Now, what are you talking about?"

"Maybe nothing." Ken shrugged sheepishly. "But it's too fishy not to consider."

"Consider what?"

"Well, you know, I used to go to this place called Ricky Roads, it's down in the flats in Chicago. It's the biggest, most beautiful strip club I ever saw."

His fifty-nine-year-old eyes glistened, savoring the memory as he spoke, smiling and carrying on as though this weren't a discussion about a man's death, but a vehicle to access past glories.

Jackie's voice came over the radio.

"Conductor 180 to the Assistant Conductor, over."

"Shit." She grabbed her radio mic. "Assistant Conductor 180."

"*Unlock-the-door.*"

"Hold that thought, Ken, and don't say anything around Jackie."

"O.K.," Ken replied, beaming with groundless self-importance.

She stood and walked to the rear door of the car. Jackie waited patiently, or at least looked that way, on the other side.

"Sorry. Got caught up with Ken. You know how he is once he gets your ear."

"Yeah," Jackie replied, repulsed, barely glancing into the car. "I'll meet you in the café. I didn't know what was going on."

Sheri felt relief; after all, it was a great opportunity for Jackie to yell at her: She had disobeyed an order.

"O.K., Jackie. I'll be right behind you."

The Conductor nodded and turned to head back to the café. "Don't leave your hat in there, either."

"O.K." Sheri locked the door and plopped back down across from Ken. "You were saying?"

"O.K. So anyway, this place was great. All the dancers had their own spots that they danced on… circles, some three feet off the ground, some five, two….."

"O.K." Sheri said impatiently.

"And the food was cheap and out of this world. So I would go there to eat, ya know?"

She rolled her eyes. "Ken, I think you're off the subject."

"No, I'm not. No, I'm not. Just listen."

She looked at her watch.

"Well, I can't listen for too long. We're gonna be in Hudson in ten minutes."

"O.K. So, I was there two nights a week for about a year--and I made friends with a few of the girls, and they started sneaking me dinners for free! It was great. So one of the girls asked if she could hitch a ride to New York. I said sure; I mean, who the hell would care? There were always empty seats. *Why not help, right*?" He looked at her with mistrust.

"I don't care who you gave rides to, Ken. It's none of my business."

He nodded, satisfied.

"So, long story longer, I started riding two girls a week, back and forth. They always insisted on having a sleeper and it was always different girls each week. Well," Ken said, his tone becoming darker. "I got worried because the spotters were riding a lot of the trains, so I told the last two that I wasn't doing it anymore… that if I got caught giving rides, I'd get fired.

"The next time I went to the club, two guys came over and sat down across from me. The younger of the two, big guy with silver sunglasses, just sat there like a bodyguard or something, and the older one says: 'You've been eatin' my Porterhouses and shrimp and drinkin' my Johnny Walker Black free--for months. Who's gonna pay for that?'

"Well, I didn't just fall off the turnip truck, right? These guys weren't joking around." Ken's face changed. He became uncomfortable the more he spoke.

"And?" Sheri prodded.

"Well, I said 'Oh, I thought the girls just liked me.' The guys looked at me like I was some kind of loser or somethin.'

"The older one laughs and says 'Listen, we had an arrangement here,' and the other guy takes a string or something out of his pocket and starts playing with it. Real creepy. I said, 'No, we didn't,' and then the old one says, 'You're taking our girls back and forth to the city--that's the end of it.'"

"And? And?" Sheri prodded.

"And--nothing. I said O.K., and got the hell outta there--and never went back. They were running something… and I bet they still are. Drugs--cash…don't know--don't want to." He laughed uncomfortably, eyes wide.

"Through strippers?"

"Yeah, girls."

"One-eighty, clear signal 115, arriving Hudson, track two," the Engineer called over the radio.

"Shit!" Sheri jumped up, grabbed her hat, and ran through the train as she heard Jackie answer.

"Rear of number four."

"Roger that, rear of four," the Engineer replied.

The train became steady as it slowed, coming into the Hudson station.

Hard to believe this was almost the capital of New York, Sheri thought as she opened the door and trap stairs as they rolled past the cliff embankment to a stop in front of the station.

She climbed down the stairs and onto the small platform, ticket punch in hand.

Jackie, who was already out there, raised her hand. "Get 'em out here. I'm not chasin' anyone today."

"O.K."

"All tickets out please! All tickets!" Sheri yelled.

The two quickly collected and punched the fifteen people's tickets and were back onboard in under their two- minute allotted station time.

Sheri closed the trap stairs and door and immediately headed toward Jackie who was now in the café car.

The Conductor was sitting on the river-side table by the window. Sheri tossed her hat on the seat and sat down, arms folded across her chest. Jackie looked out the window at the lighthouse in the middle of the river, realizing as they reached, then passed, eighty miles per hour that they had to be dealing with some sort of organized crime family.

"You know," Jackie reasoned, "If these guys are coming after us for three grand, you pissed them off somehow, Sher, and you've got to fix this. The guy drove all the way to my house in a friggin' Hummer over three grand? It just doesn't make sense. Three grand couldn't even buy the suit he was wearing."

"I know it doesn't, but that's all that happened, honestly."

"Give it back then. I'll be with you. Just say you found it--it was an innocent mistake, you thought it was abandoned."

"Yeah, that sounds reasonable enough…" the Assistant trailed off, then couldn't help herself. "I don't want to work anymore," she blurted.

"Where the hell did that come from?"

"I'm serious. Look at us. You spending every cent to rebuild a house that holds nothing but bad memories. And my basement apartment, uggh. It's like… that's it. We're stuck like this."

The Conductor glanced at her friend, then back out over the Hudson.

"If you're not happy, that's fine." Jackie said blankly. "But don't sit there making judgments about my house--you don't know anything about it."

"All you did was make yourself a prisoner to *all of it*," Sheri grunted under her breath.

"It's all I need," Jackie said flatly.

"It's not all you need," Sheri huffed.

Jackie closed her eyes. "This land that you're living in, Sher, just doesn't…really exist."

"It doesn't have to be like this, Jackie. Let's just leave here. I like your treasure-hunting idea…" Sheri grasped for a magnificent ending to her thought, but nothing came.

"I'm not going to just take off, Sher. That's completely irresponsible. The treasure-hunting thing was a joke, don't you realize that?"

"So is living for a house."

"I'm not living for my house."

"Fine… O.K.," Sheri challenged. "Since Steve left, what makes you happy about the house?"

Jackie contemplated the Assistant's question. As the seconds turned to minutes, Jackie's face grew warm with discomfort as she realized the memory of Steve had permeated every room like the stench of a dead animal, or bad pork ribs.

Sheri could see the horrible truth warm over Jackie's face like a death.

"I'm sorry…" Sheri began softly.

Jackie cut her off. "Not all parts of being an adult are fun, Sher, but I have no regrets."

"That's crap, Jackie," Sheri accused. "You don't regret Steve?"

"You don't just toss away everything you've ever worked for over another person's mistakes."

"You could find someone else and move on," Sheri countered.

"Like you found someone else?" Jackie snapped.

"I'm not going there," Sheri said flatly. Her eyes gained a hazy quality as she looked out over the river.

"Nope," Jackie agreed. "You never do go there… I mean, wherever *there* is."

She waited, but Sheri continued to stare out the window.

"But I'll tell you what…" Jackie continued sarcastically. "I'd love to visit *there* sometime. Must be a great planet. Hey, I know! Forget your career, forget everything you have. We'll send out letters to eight people and if we each send them a buck…"

"That's enough." Sheri cut her off.

"…you take off the bottom name and replace it with yours…" Jackie laughed condescendingly.

Sheri stood up from the table.

"You know something? At least I have the courage to consider there is another life out there, instead of chaining myself to ghosts."

She looked down at Jackie. The Conductor sat quietly.

"But you? You? I feel sorry for you: You're living for a house that has as many happy memories for you as the friggin' Amityville Horror house. Worse? You won't admit it. Won't even admit it to yourself. And you can't afford to leave it. Shit, how long did you have to *save up* for Caroline's the other night, Jackie? Well, I'm sorry… maybe we are on different planets, maybe you should visit mine sometime."

"Not likely," the Conductor said, putting her hat back on and standing up from the table, eye to eye with her partner.

"I don't need a rootless existence. I'm traveling five hundred miles a day, five days a week, on the way back to Albany--*I'm getting tired.*"

Jackie paused, agitated, pulling the radio off her belt. "*You, apparently--get stupid.*

"Rear of 180 to the head end," Jackie grumbled into the mic, eyes bored as they shifted away from Sheri's.

"Head end of 180, Jackie," the Engineer called back.

"Both ends of number four, Mike."

"Roger, both ends of four. Train number 180, clear signal CP 89, arriving Rhinecliff, track two."

Sheri now stood blocking the vestibule doors, arms folded in front of her chest.

"We're here, *Sherrr*," Jackie hissed.

"I'm looking at an eighty-year-old, bitter woman," Sheri said, dropping her arms and looking the Conductor up and down. "That's sad."

Jackie pushed her aside. "That's right, Sher," the Conductor replied, walking to the door. "If you don't have something, you just steal it. *Yeah*, I'm sad all right."

"From who?" Sheri yelled, as she walked through the coach. "Who did I steal from?"

Jackie wouldn't turn around.

As the train came to a stop at the station, Sheri threw open the door and stairs, bounding down the steps and onto the ground.

She whipped past the people getting on, heading straight for Jackie as she collected tickets on the platform.

"It was in a cushion! A cushion! I didn't steal from anyone!" Sheri yelled, ignoring the passengers, who stared at her as they collected their ticket receipts and climbed up the stairs onto the train.

"Still stealing," Jackie replied flatly.

"From wh--…"

"Was it yours?!?" Jackie demanded loudly. Their hats touched, bill to bill.

"It wasn't anyone's!"

"Do we really have to go over this one again?" Jackie asked with a grimace.

"Well, the person who hid it certainly didn't want to get caught with it!" Sheri said.

"Didn't that tell you something *right* there?!?" Jackie asked in bewilderment as Sheri closed her eyes and then turned and walked back to her door.

Climbing onto the train and heading for the café, she could hear Jackie call the Engineer.

"Rear of 180 to the head end, O.K. to highball Rhinecliff."

"180 has the highball, roger."

Jackie stormed back to the café.

"So where are the tickets from the people that got on at your door?" she thundered at Sheri.

Sheri sat, eyes closed, nibbling her thumbnail.

"Well?" Jackie persisted.

"Go find them yourself," Sheri said angrily, and looked back down at the table. Jackie stood staring down at her.

"I don't need this shit, Jackie. Train's yours. I'm going to the down car. Write me up…put in a complaint with management--I really don't give a shit."

Sheri walked past. The Conductor watched in silence, teeth clenched.

CHAPTER 10

Jackie sat down at the table and pulled a Tupperware container holding a grapefruit out of her bag. As she began peeling off pieces of skin, the citrus scent wafted off the juicy fruit, filling the café car.

By the time she looked up, Scorsese was sitting across from her. The blackness in his eyes made sense to her now. He carried death with him and it was staring at her. Apparently, the jury still out.

"Can I help you?" she asked him uncomfortably.

"You can help us both," he replied judiciously. His black eyes were huge, like a shark's, consuming her very being.

"Help us both?" Jackie repeated, confounded.

"Yeah, that's right. That house you got, it workin' for you O.K.?"

"What about my house?" she asked, confused.

"What--so you can't even thank me? You think I got time for your games? So, how you want to work it off then? On your back or your knees?"

Scorsese plopped his right arm across the top of the bench and stared angrily at her. She could feel herself start to tremble.

"Sir, you're making me very uncomfortable. I don't know who you are, but please return to your seat before…"

"*Before-what-you-fuckin'-bitch*," he growled. Jackie stared at him, in shock.

"Well, hello there," Mark chuckled, sliding into the seat next to Jackie, his piercing eyes locking onto Scorsese's.

Jackie's legs and hands were shaking. Mark glanced briefly at Jackie, then back toward the man.

"So, you met my friend Jimmy?" he asked, glancing at her.

"I don't know him," she replied softly.

Mark placed his hand firmly on Jackie's thigh under the table.

"*What?* FBI so broke ya gotta take the trains now?" Jimmy chuckled.

Jackie whipped her neck to the right and glared at Mark.

Mark went on, "So what are you talking to my friend about, Jim? You know this is my *friend,* right?" Mark's hand stayed firmly on her thigh as he spoke.

"Nah… nah," Jimmy replied uncomfortably. "I didn't know that."

Jimmy looked at her and then back at Mark and grinned. "We were just discussin' that it's hard when friends die suddenly."

Jackie looked up at him, shaken, as she thought of Tyrone.

"I can agree with that," Mark said, contemplating the dangerous man. "But I didn't know a guy like you had any friends."

Mark smiled at him. His confidence made Jackie feel better but she was still trembling. Gently taking his hand from Jackie's thigh, he rose from the table, the Glock clearly visible in the front of his waistband.

He motioned for Jackie to get up. Her palms were sweating as she struggled to slide herself toward the outside of the booth.

Jimmy grabbed her hand and squeezed it. Mark quickly leaned over him; one hand on the table, the other behind Jimmy's left shoulder.

"You put your *fucking* hands on her *ever*… and I do mean *ever*, again…"

"*What?*" Jimmy heckled, unafraid, yet immediately releasing Jackie's sweaty hand.

"Just saying my good-byes. That a crime now? You guys are fuckin' paranoid," he finished with a huff.

"Um-hm." Mark nodded at him. "And if I get paranoid about you, Jimmy," Mark whispered, "then I'm going to have to watch you more closely-- aren't I?"

"Sheesh," Jimmy grunted, rising from the table. "You guys are somethin'."

Jackie stood behind Mark, peering over his shoulder at Jimmy.

"Hey, Conducta!" he heckled. "I wanna complain about this bozo botherin' me and you not doin' nothin' about it. Who do I call?"

"Keep walking," Mark said flatly, and turned to face Jackie. "What's the next stop?" he asked her coldly.

"Poughkeepsie," Jackie answered softly.

"Are you opening this door here?" he asked as he pointed out into the vestibule.

"Yes," she whispered. Mark nodded at her and went through the train toward the man.

"Conductor to the Assistant, over," Jackie called over the radio quickly.

"What?" Sheri replied coldly.

"Stay up in the down car and lock yourself in."

No answer.

"Conductor to the A/C. Did you copy that?!?" Jackie yelled into the mic.

"Yeah," Sheri called back.

"What's that all about?" Ken asked, amused.

"She's on the rag," Sheri replied, and looked back out the window.

"Ya know…" Ken began, "in all my years on the railroad I've learned that your partner out here is like a spouse. Ya got a bad marriage, ya get out, ya know?"

"It's O.K. We're fine," Sheri said, lighting a cigarette as the train came to a stop on the Poughkeepsie platform.

Mark led Jimmy off the train and then got back on; Jackie called the Engineer.

"O.K. to highball Poughkeepsie."

"Roger, highball Poughkeepsie," the Engineer called back.

Looking out the window at Jimmy as the train began to move, the large man sitting in a coach seat took a small wire out of his coat pocket and began to twist it between his fingers.

Jimmy stared at Jackie, now standing in the doorway, as the train rolled by him. He nodded at her as she closed the door and turned around. Mark stood inches from her face.

"Do you want to get yourself killed, Jackie?" he asked angrily. "That's where this is heading, you know… quickly."

"Listen," Jackie replied, her face flushed, "I don't know what's happening."

Mark locked eyes with her.

"I know you took the money--I understand why you did it and how it probably happened. But the rest of it, you have to get rid of it. And I don't care *what* you do with it. But if *this guy* or any of his crew finds you buying anything outside of your means, you're just going to disappear one day, if that's not already his plan."

Jackie looked at him in disbelief.

"Mark," she began defensively, "Where do you get off telling me I'm a thief?"

"Don't toy with me," Mark countered. "I know about that huge payment you just made. Twenty thousand dollars, was it? But for some reason, they're still not sure you have it…or you'd be in fifteen pieces by now, believe me."

"That was a mistake my bank made."

"What?" he asked, agitated.

"My bank, it was a computer error. My account's always been up to date."

"Interesting," Mark replied, looking into the café and noting Sheri's workbags. "Where's your partner?"

"Oh," she answered, "in the first car."

He studied her eyes briefly and then walked past her into the café car, seating himself at the very rear table, hands clasped lightly in front of him. He sat looking at her as she stood in the aisle.

"Is Sheri in some kind of trouble?" she asked from across the café.

"Well," he began, glancing out over the Hudson as the train raced over the rails, "offhand, I'd have to say *you're* the only one in trouble."

Jackie threw her hands in the air. "Why?" she yelled, then lowered her voice. "I don't understand what I did wrong. I don't know that guy. All I know is he wanted a sleeper when he boarded the train in Schenectady the other day, and now he's showing up everywhere looking for… I don't know what. He said he lost something."

Mark regarded the fingernails on his right hand a moment, and then looked at her blankly.

"Yeah, he lost around two hundred thousand dollars, we believe."

Jackie winced. "Two hundred--"

"...thousand dollars." Mark finished her sentence.

"Well, I wasn't even in those sleepers, Mark. Why me? It's a crew of like… nine people. Why? Because I'm the Conductor?"

"No, because his money paid for your foreclosure issue and if he hasn't put it together yet, he will soon enough."

"I told you before, Mark, the bank…"

"No," Mark replied, cutting her off. "You had Sheri's attorney brother take care of it. Don't treat me like an idiot, Jackie. I'm not going to take you in, it's not like you stole from a nursing home."

"What?" Jackie asked confused.

"I'm not going to arrest you."

"No," Jackie said. "What about Sheri's brother? He's a lawyer?"

Mark looked up at the ceiling of the car, then stood up and walked over to her.

"You know something?" he said as he approached her, tipping his head slightly to the side. "When I met you the other day in that dump, I liked your act."

He looked down at the floor, shaking his head, and then looked into her eyes. "And ya know, the money… I didn't even care that you took it. I know he left it somewhere and you found it. I can't even say that, in your position, I wouldn't have done the same. But I just protected you and you're still lying to me. *You're* no better than *he* is."

Jackie's eyes began to water as the pieces fit together and she realized what Sheri had done for her. "Well, I guess I'm the bad guy then, right?" Jackie asked, trying to blink the mist from her eyes.

"Yup," Mark replied, disappointed. "You *are* the bad guy."

Jackie stared at him, hurt, and grabbed the radio off her belt. "Conductor 180 to the head end, over."

Mark stood watching her in their stalemate.

"Head end 180," the Engineer answered.

"Bring the train to a safe stop at the next Metro North station."

"That'll be New Hamburg, Jackie," the Engineer called back.

"New Hamburg, roger." She looked at Mark.

"Ever been to New Hamburg?" the Conductor asked.

He shook his head as the train began to slow.

"O.K., well…now you can say you have been." Jackie walked to the door and slid it open as the train stopped, stepping aside as Mark reluctantly stepped off onto the platform and put his black sunglasses back on.

"Remember the other night," Jackie asked as she pulled the radio off her hip. "After Caroline's, when you called me?… Highball 180," she called over the radio as she waited for Mark's reply.

"Roger, highball," the Engineer called back and, with two toots of the horn, the train began to move.

"Yeah," Mark replied, looking at her confused as the train rolled away.

"I didn't believe you, either." Jackie closed the door.

Feeling dejected as the train arrived on the platform at Penn Station in New York City, Jackie snapped to just long enough to key the coach doors open. *What have you done now, Sheri?* she whispered, gathering up the tickets and trip report.

Sheri returned to the café car just as Jackie was getting off the train. The Conductor's eyes regarded her coldly. She walked by the Assistant without uttering a word.

Sheri walked into the empty café and sat at a table, staring at her bags. "*Shit,*" she mumbled, looking inside. She had left the two bottles of wine in her workbag. She quickly hid them under her railroad rule books.

Getting her things together, she plopped her backpack on top of her roller bag as she stepped off the train. She stopped and lit a cigarette, noticing the OUT OF SERVICE sign still on the track elevator.

"Three weeks…this place is ridiculous," she huffed, taking another drag and flicking the ashes toward the NO SMOKING sign on the pillar.

Taking the escalator to the main floor, she made her way by the hordes of people, National Guardsmen, dogs, and wheelchairs to the escalator that would bring her back down to the crew room. It was located on the station's middle level, where one should be if one were looking for the subway or Long Island Rail Road trains.

She rolled her bag into the crew room. The conductors yelled back and forth to one another as though standing next to a diesel engine. Actually, there was no call for that, as the room measured only thirty by thirty feet.

Sheri covered her ears as one of the conductors screamed as she passed by. Annoyed, she focused on the Albany crew table and Jackie, who stood staring at her. The Conductor finally turned her glare away as she placed her hat and radio into her workbag.

Ken stood at the far end of the crew room, sheepishly regarding the two of them.

Bill Archeddy walked over to Jackie. "Are you my conductor on 139 today?" the Engineer asked.

"Yeah, that's me," Jackie answered with a forced smile.

"O.K.," the Engineer replied warmly. "I'll see you back here at sign-up."

"Great." Jackie nodded and walked over to Sheri. "Are you getting something to eat?" the Conductor asked.

"Yeah," Sheri answered.

Ken called over to Sheri. "You're working 139?"

"Yeah," Sheri called back.

"C'mere, c'mere," Ken waved her over toward the quieter portion of the crew room, as he leaned on one of the green recliners. Jackie and Sheri walked over to him.

"I called Sheri," Ken said quietly.

"I'm the Conductor on 139," Jackie replied, pissed off.

"*And* I was talking to *Sheri*," Ken retorted, eyes wide.

"Whatever, Ken," Jackie said. "I'll meet you in the hall," she said looking at Sheri, and walked out of the room.

"Ken, you can't talk to her like that," Sheri warned.

"She's got thick skin. So listen, you working 139 regular now? Every week then?" he asked.

Sheri nodded.

"Well," he continued, "since talking to you on the way here, I was thinking about where they hide whatever they're runnin', and it's got to be either the cushions or the vents."

Sheri looked down at the floor.

"Maybe there," he speculated, "but it also could be the electrical cabinet in the baggage car…." He trailed off.

"What?" Sheri asked, looking up.

"Yeah, the electrical cabinet in the baggage car. They all have that old, dirty shelf. You know where I'm talking about?"

"Yeah, I think so," Sheri replied, trying to visualize. "But, why there?" she asked.

"Well, I used to bring the girls in there to smoke, and after a while, they'd go in on their own." His face turned a nice shade of pink as he grinned, embarrassed, and continued. "And you know I don't smoke but, well ya have to check on 'em. What if they fell or something in there? Oh boy, could you just imagine me tryin' to explain two six-foot blonds, in leather and wearing pink go-go boots in the baggage car?" he said with a roll of his eyes.

"What are you saying?" Sheri asked.

"They were always, always, always over by the electrical locker. I never thought anything of it until now."

Sheri shrugged. "Why would they put anything there?"

"So it can't be tied to 'em if it's found." Ken replied.

"Why are you telling me this?" Sheri finally asked.

"Because you can check, and take it! It's like limbo loot!"

"I've got a strange feeling it doesn't work like that, Ken," she replied quickly. "I have to get going."

"Oh, O.K." Ken waved his hands discontentedly. "You kids have no sense of adventure these days." He walked away in a huff.

Sheri walked out into the hall. Jackie was staring off into space at the departure boards.

"I know, I know," Jackie said. "Good ol' Ken."

"Burgers?" Sheri asked.

"O.K.," Jackie replied, looking down at her watch. "We only have another hour before we're back on duty anyway."

The conductors walked through Penn Station, weaving in and out of the hustle and bustle as they made their way to a burger joint they liked. Jackie suddenly froze in the middle of the hall. A large black woman banged into her as she stopped. She looked at Jackie and sucked her teeth then continued by. Sheri stopped and turned around.

"How close are you to starting that treasure-hunting business?" Jackie asked.

"The what?" Sheri asked, stunned.

"Thanks for taking care of the house," Jackie said looking in her eyes.

"I don't understand," Sheri replied worriedly.

"Sheri. You have gotten us so deep in shit… I don't think there's any way out."

Sheri quickly walked up next to her. "Everything's fine. It's O.K.," she reassured. "I'm going to give it back."

"You can't now. It's too late." Jackie looked up at the ceiling. "Two hundred thousand dollars sound about right?"

"Two-fifty," Sheri replied softly. "Maybe a little more."

Jackie winced and closed her eyes.

"I kept it because I wanted to save your house…" Sheri said weakly.

"I know why you did it, Sher, and I love you for it… but if I could have you take it back I would, you know." Jackie stared deeper into her eyes. "I would."

"I know," Sheri replied, glancing at the floor while a continuous flow of people passed by them from every which way. "I didn't know if they were stacks of twenties or hundreds or just mixed, I didn't know what I needed. I just… I never saw anything like it and I just… I just…"

"We'll figure this thing out," Jackie reassured, placing her arm around Sheri's shoulder. "You don't have a selfish bone in your body, Sher, that much I know. C'mon, let's get a burger, Bonnie."

Sheri smiled affectionately. "Oh, so you're automatically Clyde? That's ridiculous."

"But that's the way it is," Jackie shrugged.

They ate their lunch in the silence of the truce. Jackie thought about Mark and the irony. The first man to catch her eye in what seemed like forever, and he saw her as "the bad guy."

"A criminal," she muttered through a chuckle.

"I'm not a criminal," Sheri huffed as she dipped a French fry into the mayo/mustard blob oozing from her half-eaten burger.

"Mark and Alan aren't married," Jackie said, looking up at her and dabbing her mouth with the napkin as she spoke.

Sheri stared quietly. "No?"

"Nope. They're FBI agents."

"Ooooooh shhhhit," Sheri whispered, setting her burger down. "How do you know that?"

"It's a long story, but believe me when I tell you, this money thing is gonna get ugly."

"Ugly, how?"

"Mark said those guys are going to kill us, and chop us into little pieces."

Sheri swallowed hard and stared down at her rare, half-eaten burger.

"Pieces," she whispered.

"Yup," Jackie replied calmly. "Tiny, tiny pieces."

"This is all your fault," Sheri said, glaring at Jackie and picking up her burger, hands trembling.

"*My* fault?" Jackie repeated angrily. "Yeah, Sher… you'll inform me when the shuttle lands."

"Well, it is! It's that stupid house! They're *dead*--and it doesn't matter how long you work on it, *they- aren't-coming-back*. You're obsessed…" She trailed off. "I'm sorry, Jackie." Sheri composed herself and looked at her friend. "I didn't mean it."

"No, you're right, Sher," Jackie replied as she pushed the plate away. "I don't want to be like a fifty-year-old pop star someday, obsessing about my nose and filling the house with mannequins."

She snickered, but Sheri could see the pain in her eyes.

"Hey," Sheri said, "why don't we take a leave of absence, take a long trip somewhere? Margaritas on the beach?"

For the first time, Sheri could see Jackie was thinking about it.

"They'll follow us," Jackie replied softly.

"Oh, a little excitement in an otherwise boring life," Sheri offered with a grin.

Both women's eyes were tearing up; they sat looking at each other.

"Do you think it's like in the movies when they chop people up and put them in cement, or bakery freezers?" Sheri asked, toying, trying to cover her fear.

"Nah, people are lazy nowadays. They probably just shoot you and drop ya off at the dump." Jackie shivered. "Let's go sign up for work," the Conductor said, looking at her watch.

They made their way back through the station to the sign-up room. The two conductors walked down the narrow hallway toward the glass partition. Jackie reached into the small opening in the glass and grabbed the Albany crew assignment sheet. No less than three managers were standing nearby.

"Not good," Jackie said.

"Hi," one of the managers greeted. "You guys out of Albany?"

"Yeah," Jackie answered. "What's goin' on?"

"One of the transformers is on fire in the tunnel, so you're not going anywhere anytime soon."

"Cool," Sheri chirped.

Jackie put her hands on her hips nervously.

"You guys don't have to hang out here in the station; just give me your cell number and we'll call you when we start clearing this mess up."

"That sounds great," Jackie replied, taking her cell phone from her pocket. Her incoming text light was on. Jackie flipped the phone open.

A text message flashed: DO NOT GET ON TRAIN 139.

"Mark?" Jackie murmured.

She texted him back. AND WHY NOT?

She pressed SEND, finished giving the manager her number, and motioned for Sheri to come out into the hall. The phone beeped again.

THEY'VE ORDERED THE HIT ON YOU BOTH. I REPEAT: DO NOT GET ON TRAIN 139.

Jackie closed the phone and looked up at Sheri, who was searching her face.

"You're white as a ghost, Jack," she whispered worriedly. "What's wrong?"

"It was Mark," Jackie replied, stunned. "He said we're gonna get…what's the word they use? Whacked? We're gonna get whacked if we get on 139 tonight."

"What?!" Sheri cried out.

"Do you have any money?" Jackie asked worriedly.

"I did before we got lunch. You know I don't carry much down here."

"I know, neither do I. We have to get on 139." Jackie said apprehensively. "There's no choice. We can't ask anyone here to help, they'll know we're taking off."

"Hey, wait a second, though." Sheri's face brightened. "Maybe we won't even get out of here for a few hours… Maybe they'll get paranoid and leave."

"That's a good point. Let's go over to the day room at the hotel until the manager calls," Jackie said, looking around the hall.

Sheri nodded. "Let's go."

The conductors quickly bounded the stairs to the main level, hurriedly walking under the departure board and past the waiting area.

They went around to the right by the coffee shop, pizza place, and some pervy underwear store out onto Seventh Avenue at the Madison Square Garden side.

"Do you think it could take more than an hour or two for us to get out of here?" Sheri looked around, then side to side. So many people; her head was spinning. They both stopped, hearing a man yelling. They looked to the right a little ways down the street, where a man was weaving in and out on the sidewalk with a three foot piece of cardboard draped over his head yelling: "I WAN-CHU—-TA LEE-ME-DAFUCK ALONE," over and over again.

"Yeah," Jackie said while looking across the street, waiting for the WALK sign. "Do the math: They gotta put the fire out, clear the smoke, backed up trains… it'll be ten o'clock tonight before we get out of here."

Sheri's face brightened. "You're right." The signal changed and they walked across the street.

"I feel so paranoid," Sheri said as they walked through the revolving door into the Penn Plaza hotel.

"Hi," Sheri greeted the stout Asian woman behind the glass partition.

"Day woom, wight?" The woman asked. Jackie nodded. The woman pulled up a large black binder reading *1409* in two-inch letters and slid it to them from under the glass.

Jackie scribbled her name, took a room card key from the small white envelope, and passed the binder toward the Assistant. Sheri scribbled her initials.

They walked through the large, marbled lobby toward the elevators. A chunky white man with red hair sat at the security booth, checking to ensure that people had room keys before they proceeded to the elevators. He seemed more interested in his dinner. Sheri watched him hold his black plastic plate in his left hand and shovel mashed potatoes and peas into his mouth with the other. He glanced at them momentarily and then shoveled in another scoop.

"I feel safe," Jackie said sarcastically as she pressed the UP button on the wall.

"Tell me about it," Sheri snorted as they stepped into the elevator and pressed the button for 14. CNN was broadcasting on a tiny screen in the upper-left portion of the wall: MAN KILLS FAMILY, SELF was the tagline.

"I need some good news," Jackie said with a sigh.

"I just want to get to the room right now," Sheri replied as the elevator door opened again.

They walked down the long hallway to 1409, the crew day room.

Jackie stuck the plastic card key into the lock and pushed the heavy door open. They walked inside and peered around the large, uninhabited room.

On the far right side of the room, a 17-inch TV stood, too small for viewing from any of the seats. The room also boasted three large leather couches and a coffee table. Behind one couch sat a large glass dining table about seven feet long surrounded by several mismatched metal chairs. A large reclining chair sat in front of one window; a third couch was pushed up against the far wall. The commercial-grade carpet, an old tan-and-orange print, had cigarette burns near the window. The bathroom was located in a separate room, right behind the TV, but its window would open only about two inches, as though this were a casino hotel.

Sheri pulled a cigarette from her shirt pocket and fished for her lighter in her pants pocket.

"You're not going to sit here chain-smoking, are ya?" the Conductor asked.

"Let's see…" Sheri began, looking at the cigarette a moment. "We're supposed to die today. Hmm… Yup, I'll be chain-smoking." Sheri lit the cigarette, blew the smoke out and stared blankly at Jackie.

Jackie nodded as Sheri plopped down on the recliner by the window.

"No one's going to get on the train." Sheri added, taking another drag and flicking the ashes onto the windowsill.

"I hope not," Jackie replied as she handed Sheri a Styrofoam cup half filled with water. "Use this."

"I don't mind the window."

"Just use it," Jackie snapped.

Sheri shrugged and took the cup.

Jackie folded her arms across her chest. "You know, Sher, we're done if those people do get on 139. There's nowhere to hide on a train."

The Conductors locked eyes knowingly.

"We just have to keep our fingers crossed that we leave really late," Sheri said, lowering her gaze to the cup in her hand and dropping the butt in it with a hiss.

"Even if we get to Albany, what then?" Jackie asked. "They know where we live; we already know that, so what do we do when we get there? I mean, are they going to be at the station, our houses…" She trailed off.

"We're in trouble, aren't we?" Sheri asked her partner softly.

"We're in huge trouble."

"Call Mark, Jack," Sheri said anxiously. "He'll help us."

"That can't happen either, Sher."

"Why nnn…"

Jackie cut her off. "He thinks I took the money because of the foreclosure."

"WHAT?" Sheri yelled.

"Well, think about it… it's not like you went out and bought yourself a new car with cash. But suddenly my twenty thousand dollar delinquency is gone? He assumes it's me."

"Well, he assumes wrong. Call him, I'll tell him everything." Sheri stood up and held her hand out for the cell phone.

Jackie looked down at the phone. "No. I'm not kissing the ass of someone who wants to think of me like that. He's not on our side, Sher, and I don't feel like explaining this to a room full of F.B.I. guys, do you?"

"It's better than what might happen to us…" Sheri pointed out.

"Is it?" Jackie asked. "Think, Sher. First, we'd be fired. Now, that's assuming we live, but we'll be fired for not turning the money over, or reporting it. Then, there's a chance we'd be thrown in jail."

"We're not going to jail," Sheri mocked.

"They'd think of something, trust me. It wasn't like it was a dime…two hundred and fifty thousand dollars-- and you took it *home*? Bullshit. I'll take my chances."

"Well, if they're on the train, maybe we could tell them where it is… Scorsese, I mean," Sheri offered.

"Actually, the guy's name is Jimmy something. Anyway, Mark said a hit has already been put out on us for this. These people don't *change their minds*," Jackie shook her head.

"How about asking Mark to put us in witness protection?"

Jackie sighed, agitated. "Sheri, you watch too much TV. You're not a witness, you're a thief."

Sheri looked at her, hurt.

"Lookit," Jackie said calmly, "That's to protect people who testify against these guys in court. We have nothing to offer anyone. This is one of those 'you've made your own bed' things. We're alone. You need to warm up to that fact… and quickly."

"What if they attack us on the train?" Sheri asked.

"Well, I'm pretty sure, whoever they are, they're gonna avoid doing it in front of witnesses, so we gotta try to stay around people." Jackie hesitated. "I don't know how they're going to do it," she said, shaking her head.

Sheri sat down on the recliner and rested her head against the cushion. "Do you want to know why I left Matt?" Sheri asked, looking up at the ceiling.

Jackie quickly cut her off. "No. You never told me before, and you wouldn't be now if you weren't giving up. We'll get through this, Sher. Toughen up."

"I'm gonna take a nap until the station calls," Sheri said, depressed, getting up and walking behind Jackie to one of the couches.

"How the hell can you sleep?" Jackie asked in disbelief.

"I don't feel too good," Sheri admitted.

"I know," Jackie conceded. "My stomach's drilling holes in itself."

"Well, read a magazine or something then. You've got a signal in here, right?" Sheri asked.

Jackie flipped the phone open. "Yeah, I do." She walked to the other couch on the opposite side of the room from Sheri, kicked her shoes off, set her cell phone on top of the coffee table, and lay back on the couch, a copy of *Architectural Digest* in her hand.

The layout of the train played over and over in her mind. *Engine, baggage car, three sleeper cars, the diner, the café, and then four coaches.*

"There's nowhere to hide," she murmured as she flipped mindlessly through the pages.

CHAPTER 11

A few hours and many outdated issues of *The Enquirer* later, Sheri glanced around the room to the window. A large pile of cigarette ashes had accumulated next to her on the floor. It was dark outside. She stretched for a moment, then got up and walked over to Jackie, who was staring at the ceiling. She picked up Jackie's cell phone quietly and looked at the time. It read: 8:37 AND NO MISSED CALLS.

She set the phone back on the table and walked over to the coffee pot. She could hear Jackie mumbling as she bravely poured them each a cup of the old coffee.

"What time is it?" Jackie asked from across the room.

"It's after eight-thirty," Sheri answered, turning on the light and handing her the stale coffee.

Jackie's phone beeped as Sheri lit another cigarette. She opened the cell.

THAT FIRE SAVED YOUR LIFE. 139 IS CANCELLED. PLEASE CALL ME WHEN YOU ARRIVE BACK IN ALBANY TOMORROW, WE'LL TALK.

Jackie laughed.

"What?" Sheri asked.

"That was Mark. He said our train's *cancelled*, and to let him know when we're back *tomorrow*."

Sheri spit her coffee out.

"Hey," Jackie chuckled, "we can always hope Jimmy and crew know as little about these trains."

"Don't they know yet that it can be twelve hours late--and *still* go?" Sheri heckled. "*Whyyyyy*? Because '*WE'RE not happy--until YOU'RE not happy.*'"

They laughed and sipped their coffees, noses wrinkled, Sheri again flicking her ashes on the windowsill. Jackie ignored it.

"By the time we leave, the passengers will be too tired to bitch," Jackie quipped.

"It's so evil," Sheri giggled.

"*Oooh-we're sorry it's so late*," Jackie began sarcastically, '*Please accept this mini Snickers bar as a token of our commitment to you, our passengers.*'"

"Oh," Sheri chimed in, "those little boxed lunches go over great, too. I'm surprised they don't do MREs!" They laughed uncontrollably.

"Yeah," Jackie retorted. "We should have little passenger emergency packs on every train. A brakeman's lantern, cell phone, summer sausage, and a complaint form. Yeah… with a disclaimer on top of the form: 'Please don't mistake this as meaning we give a shit.'"

"Are you going to reply to Mark?" Sheri asked, her smile fading.

"And say what?"

"I don't know," Sheri answered, frustrated.

Jackie opened the phone and wrote back: I NEVER LIED TO YOU. FURTHER, HOPEFULLY YOU KNOW MORE ABOUT YOUR JOB THAN YOU DO ABOUT TRAINS.

She set the phone back on the table.

"What did you say?" Sheri asked anxiously.

"Nothing close to what you wanted me to," Jackie replied flatly.

The phone rang; Jackie looked at the number. "It's the station," she said.

They stood and went toward the door.

"Do you think the guys that are after us waited this long for the train?" Sheri probed.

"I hope not, Sher," Jackie replied guardedly.

They closed the door behind them and headed back through the busy hotel lobby to the street.

Everything around them seemed to move in slow motion. The taxis blowing their horns, the tourists scurrying about and the people with their HELP THE HOMELESS jugs yelling to anyone who would listen; all seemed to quiet as they approached the station.

Sheri flicked her cigarette between pedestrians as they got on the escalator and descended once again into Penn Station.

They walked quickly by the bakery, deli, bank, pizza shop, and pervy underwear store once more. Using the steps by the pretzel vendor, they bypassed the passengers in the waiting area and walked through the long, empty corridor connecting the LIRR with the subway. In the sign-up room, Mitch Laraby, one of the managers, was waiting for them.

"Hello, ladies," he greeted. They could see the stress the fire had caused.

"Hi, Mitch," they replied.

"Your train is next through the tubes. It'll be about twenty minutes."

"O.K.," Jackie replied.

"Listen," the manager said, "just open all the doors, let everyone pile on, and straighten it out on the road, O.K.?"

"That's fine," Jackie nodded, unfazed.

"Oooh boy." Sheri grimaced nervously.

"The quicker we get out of here, the quicker we're off the train," Jackie snapped.

"Ooooookay. But, letting three hundred people pile on isn't making me feel too secure right now, know what I mean?" Sheri complained.

"What's the difference?" Jackie began to lose her patience. "Do you think you're going to know who they are?"

"Maybe," Sheri replied, following Jackie back out into the hallway. "I'd like to take a crack at it, and at least know where they are on my train."

"It's not gonna make a difference, Sher."

"This is ridiculous," Sheri huffed.

"Don't get me started," Jackie warned.

"I'm not getting on that train," Sheri suddenly blurted.

"Oh, yes you are. Get your bags, Sher."

"We're gonna be murdered," she said angrily to the Conductor.

"I won't let anything happen to you…I swear it," the Conductor said, looking at the Assistant. Sheri stood quietly, looking around the long hallway. Jackie waited.

"I'm afraid of being chopped into pieces," Sheri admitted in a half-whisper.

"Oh, is that all?" Jackie quipped. "They do that *after* you're dead, Sher. That's no problem."

The two began to walk across the hall to the crew room to get their workbags, Jackie leading slowly.

"I always thought they did that while you were alive," Sheri said softly, following behind the Conductor.

"Nah, that's just to hide the parts."

"Oh, O.K.," Sheri replied, somehow relieved. "I guess that's O.K."

"O.K.?" Jackie said, throwing her hands in the air as they reached the lockers. "This has been the most ridiculous week of my life!"

Removing her workbags from the wire locker and plopping them on the crew table with a thud, she faced Sheri. "C'mere." Jackie said, and nudged the Assistant to the corner of the room. "This is what we're gonna do."

Sheri stood close, listening.

"Start getting tickets in the front of the train in the sleepers, as soon as we depart, and I'll start in the rear coach, coming toward you."

Jackie took the radio out of her bag and turned it on. "Get your radio," she commanded as she turned the channels.

Sheri went through her bag, locating the radio with ease.

"Well, you can get it together when you have to," Jackie sighed. "Turn it to 7671."

Sheri turned to 7671 and looked back up.

"Now listen," Jackie continued, "when you're collecting tickets and you hear this—" she pressed the TALK button on the side of the radio three times quickly. The open wave caused a series of loud static clicks on Sheri's end.

"O.K., if I hear what?" Sheri asked impatiently.

Jackie blinked slowly, looking at the Assistant, then continued. "As I was saying, if you hear this--the static --it means to meet me in the baggage car… immediately."

"Why there?" Sheri asked.

"Because it's the only car on the train that has a heavy manual door. Worse comes to worst, we can try to hold it shut somehow. I don't know, you have something better?"

Sheri nodded. "I think you're right; at least there's room in there to move around."

"Just don't get yourself trapped, Sher. It can happen real easy."

"You think there's going to be more than one guy?" Sheri quizzed.

"Well, there's two of us. I don't know…." The Conductor trailed off. "Do you carry a knife in your bag?" Jackie suddenly asked.

"I've got a metal file," Sheri answered.

"What are you going to do? Their nails?" Jackie retorted.

"It's the closest thing to a knife that I have. It's metal, and it comes to a point," Sheri snipped defensively.

"Let's put our work stuff in the baggage car," the Conductor said.

"O.K.," Sheri acknowledged.

"Track eight," Jackie said in a daze, looking at the track-designation screen.

"Eight," Sheri repeated uneasily.

The conductors looked at one another in silence. Jackie closed her eyes and took a deep breath. "Let's go," she said, grabbing the handle of her workbag.

Sheri nodded and followed the Conductor into the hall. They walked by six small groups of people, their gaze glued to the several different TV screens showing the tracks from which each train was arriving or departing.

During the middle of the afternoon, there are a few stampedes each hour. Once a boarding announcement is made, suddenly several hundred passengers all charge toward a specific track. After seven o'clock at night, it's not so bad.

Except, of course, for tonight. A group of passengers who were supposed to stampede onto a train at three o'clock were doing it over six hours later. This would not be just *any* stampede, but a three-hundred-strong, *angry* stampede.

The conductors pressed the DOWN button on the elevator and stood waiting. As the door opened, they stood looking in apprehensively. Jackie stuck her foot out, blocking it before it could close.

She then reached over in front of Sheri and pressed the TL, or track level, button.

The elevator descended to track level. The door opened and they stepped out onto the platform. The air was stagnant and hot. The sound of the engine, held captive below the building, penetrated the entire platform like a three-thousand-pound bumble bee.

The closer they got to the baggage car, the louder the noise became. Sheri stopped and lit a cigarette; Jackie glanced at it, shaking her head as she stepped into the baggage car, and disappeared inside.

Sheri took another long puff. Her heart skipped a beat as she watched the people scrambling down onto the platform toward the rear and squeezing onto the train.

It looked like a mosh pit, she thought, blowing out the smoke and flicking the butt onto the tracks.

She quickly lifted her workbags onto the train and found Jackie inside. The Conductor was standing still, watching the Assistant approach her inside the hollow baggage car which is basically nothing more than a glorified boxcar. Metal, rusty, dirty, no frills. Its contents consisted of tagged luggage bound for Chicago, Buffalo, Syracuse…plus bicycles, someone's mountain gear, and the belongings of a passenger who was apparently moving cross country.

Sheri's bag rolled behind her; the wheels going over the rusty metal rattled like a machine gun.

She stood in front of her partner. "What?" Sheri asked.

"I feel like killing you myself right now," Jackie said, teeth clenched.

"Kill me later," Sheri offered. "The people are boarding themselves already."

"It's better that way," Jackie said. "They're just going to piss and moan. Better to get'em on first."

"Yup," Sheri nodded, and lit another cigarette.

"Jeez," Jackie said annoyed. "Do you have something against air?"

"Yeah, it happened a long time ago," Sheri quipped.

They stepped out of the baggage car and back onto the platform.

The Conductors put their hats on and walked alongside the train. Sheri stopped, taking position by the first sleeper, and Jackie continued down past the remaining two sleepers, café, and diner toward the coaches in the rear.

The majority of passengers having boarded, there was only a trickle of people left coming down the escalator.

The attendants all were out, standing by their respective doors.

Mitch Laraby was there, anxiously waiting for the gate, or the O.K. for the train to depart the station.

"Hey, Mitch," Jackie said flatly.

"Hey," he replied, without taking his eyes from the top of the escalator. A woman stood at the top, looking to one side at the clock. She abruptly looked down and waved.

"You've got the gate!" she yelled.

"O.K. Let's go. You've got it," Mitch said.

Jackie blew the whistle that hung around her neck like a piece of jewelry and waved to the attendants, who immediately disappeared inside the train. She waved to Sheri, who hopped on between the baggage car and the first sleeper car.

"Rear of 139 to the head end, over."

"Head end of 139," the Engineer called back.

Jackie took a deep breath. "O.K. to highball Penn Station, signal indication, no Form-D's."

"Roger, highball Penn Station. One-thirty-nine departing Penn Station on a clear signal," the Engineer called over the radio.

The train began to roll along the platform. Jackie turned and looked out the door window as they picked up speed. She swallowed hard and turned around, leaning against the door.

"I am going to kill her when this is over," she said composing herself, and then grabbing the ticket punch from its holster and walking quickly through all four coaches, straight past the three hundred angry bulls.

Reaching the rear of the fourth coach, Jackie immediately began collecting tickets. She was halfway through the car before she got the first complaint. Complaints on a train in this situation, Jackie knew, were like an avalanche: one little snowball or two rolls off, and the next thing you know--BAM! The whole thing falls down on top of you. *Here we go*, she thought as she listened to the seventy-something man.

"You know, we sat there for six hours and no one had the common courtesy to tell us anything," he complained.

Jackie could see his anger grow as he spoke. "And," he continued, becoming louder, "You can't tell me they didn't know it was going to be *hours* late. I don't think I should have to pay for this. This isn't customer service. It's… it's…" He hesitated, and then exploded. "This is bullshit! That's what this is!"

"Harold, Harold, stop it!" his wife ordered angrily. "She didn't do it; she's sorry for us."

"Not sorry enough!" he thundered.

Jackie stared at him. "Sir, the delay was terrible, I'm uncertain of the particulars that caused it, but I suggest you lodge your complaint through the 800 number."

The man became incensed. "Listen, lady!" he yelled.

Jackie leaned down in his ear. "I'm not your lady. I'm not some stewardess. I'm the

Conductor on this train, and I'm telling you *right now*: If you yell at me one more time, I'm gonna *throw your ass off*, and you can explain how angry you are to the cops I'll have waiting for you. Got it?"

"I told you to keep your mouth shut, Harold," his wife snipped.

"Be quiet, Helen," the man ordered, then looked up at Jackie and reluctantly nodded.

"Now listen," said Jackie, "my guess is they'll refund or compensate you in some way, but enough with the scene, O.K.--it doesn't help."

It was too late. She had only collected two more tickets before the "prairie dog syndrome" began, with heads popping up to look over the seat tops, and with it the next round of complaints.

"You people should be atta business," a fortyish woman slurred. Cigarettes and booze oozed from her.

Jackie turned her head away, sucking in as much air as possible, and turned to face her again.

"Yas know what?" the woman said, disgusted, trying to wave her hand but only managing a limp, drunken flail. "I don't like you. What's your name, Conductress?"

Jackie leaned down. "You liked that *vodka* though, didn't you?" she asked. "One more word out of *you*--and you're going to like me a lot *less*. Trust me."

"I'm not fraidayou." the woman sneered, but retreated and looked out the window.

Jackie continued through the coach. She grabbed the tickets as fast as she could. She knew the less they saw of her, the less opportunity there was to harass her.

"Excuse me, Conducta," the voice said from behind.

Jackie froze and then slowly turned around. It was him. The man stood six-feet-four, his large silver sunglasses looming over her. There was no expression on his face.

"Can I help you, sir?" Jackie asked stiffly.

"Don't matter if you can, you're gonna," the man replied as he played with a strange, small wire.

Fear raced through her; she pushed the talk button on her mic.

"What can I do for you, sir?" she said loudly, hoping Sheri would hear.

"You gotta problem--and we need someplace private to work it out." He tapped the butt of the gun lodged in his waistband. Jackie let go of the mic.

"What if we give it back?" Jackie asked, not moving from the security of the passengers.

The man gave a perverse smile, and she knew there was no way out.

"We can discuss a modification, maybe. Tell me where it is," he said flatly.

The woman sitting in the coach seat next to where Jackie stood was listening to the exchange and glanced up at her uncomfortably. The Conductor was trapped. Even if she were able to quickly make a call over the radio to get the police, it would take too long between calling the Engineer, the Engineer calling the Dispatcher, the Dispatcher calling the cops…*shhhit*.

Sheri ran frantically toward the baggage car, clenching her radio and bouncing side to side off the sleeper car walls as the train roared through the underground tunnels and deposited them into midtown Manhattan--the first leg of the Hudson Run.

Sheri raced inside, sliding the heavy metal door closed behind her.

She paced over the metal floor of the large, luggage laden boxcar. "Shit! Shit!" She called out breathlessly, her heart pounding. She held the radio up to her ear. Nothing. "Shit!"

She banged her hand against the electrical cabinet door, then stared at it.

"Ken," she said, her eyes widening. She opened the dented metal door and looked inside. Wires and switches covered one side; a brakeman's lantern hanging on a bolt and an old poster of Lynda Carter in her Wonder Woman outfit the other side. Sheri looked down at the cabinet floor: Dusty, opened first-aid kits, a crowbar, a crumpled-up comic book, and an empty pack of smokes. She kept the radio to her ear, trying to catch her breath as she looked past the wires, panel, and emergency information sheets. About a foot from the top she saw the shelf. It was too high; she couldn't see that far.

She reached up and felt around. Her hand grazed something plastic and she pulled on it. A bag fell on the floor, just missing her head.

"Why hasn't she come up here yet?" Sheri lamented worriedly as she looked inside the black bag. Jackie's voice came over the radio.

"Modify what?" she asked. Sheri could hear the fear in her voice.

"We treat the ladies who steal from us *real special*," the deep male voice said coldly.

Sheri's jaw dropped; the radio fell silent. She reached inside the electrical cabinet, grabbed the crowbar, and opened the door between the baggage car and the engine. Only a foot of space was open between the steel ends of the baggage car and locomotive; Sheri looked down at the cables between the car and engine; the swirling vacuum of the wind unnerved her as she spotted the large, blue cable two feet down.

"I've got to knock the power out," she panicked. The train was easily going seventy-five miles per hour.

She looked down at the cable, trying to ignore the hard fact of the ground whizzing below; all she could feel was wind, and all she could see was blackness.

"Shit." Carefully, crowbar in her left hand, Sheri stepped across onto the engine's back step. She straddled between the boxcar and engine, half frozen, staring down at the cable.

"This is useless," she said, tossing the crowbar back into the baggage car. "I'm gonna have to go down there… there's no other way." Her hair swirled around her face. "The only way to drop the power is to dislocate this friggin' cable."

The air pressure pushed at her from both sides equally as she lowered herself. Bending her knees until she was squatting, she balanced herself between the massive steel ends. She carefully placed her hands in front of her feet, grabbing the dirty metal foot rests as they roared past stations and buildings through Croton-Harmon.

Her arms trembled for a moment, and then she stiffened. Lifting her legs under her own strength, she began to lower herself onto the cable.

"If this thing arcs, I'm dead," she thought, looking down at the dangerous electrical cable, arms trembling as she began to bounce on it, trying to shake it loose. She turned around, grabbed the ladder that ran down the side of the engine and ended in a large metal stirrup at the bottom, and started jumping on the cable.

"Gimme a break!" she yelled angrily; sweat was being sucked off her forehead by the wind as she jumped with her full weight on it a ninth, then a tenth, time.

The cable suddenly popped out. It made an exploding sound; an arc of bright light shot by her. Sheri clenched the engine ladder handle and closed her eyes, her whole body shaking.

She opened her eyes and looked down. The cable was disconnected, most likely dragging beneath the train. She unclenched her hands and began to hoist herself up, arms shaking. She finally got one knee back on the footrest and stretched the other across to the baggage car. She rose to her feet, crossed back over, and closed the metal door between the baggage car and the engine; the car was pitch-black inside.

The door leading into the baggage car on the opposite end slid open with a crash. Sheri froze. A moment later the door slammed shut.

"What did you do? What did you do?" Jackie yelled, her voice getting closer. "Thank you! I thought he was going to shoot me right there! We have to get the hell off this train, Sher." The Conductor was within feet of Sheri now. "How did you cut the lights?" Jackie asked, out of breath.

"I disconnected the 480 cable."

"What!" Jackie yelled. "You went between the engine and the baggage car! You're nuts! Open the side door. I can't see shit in here!"

The giant, square loading door opened two feet. Jackie glanced at her assistant, then out the door toward the river. "There isn't going to be an easy answer for us," Jackie said, looking out as the train raced over the rails.

"What happened back there?" Sheri asked.

"It's a good thing you cut the power when you did. Someone thought the guy was just another complaining passenger and started yelling at me from the other side, so when the lights went out, I moved around him and ran through… Holy shit." Jackie finished, exasperated. "We're gonna have to jump, Sher," the Conductor added, "There's no choice, and no time. A train's a one-way street; he'll find his way here sooner or later."

"If we jump, we're gonna die," Sheri resisted.

"If we stay on this thing, we're gonna die… believe me," Jackie replied somberly.

Sheri moved closer to the opening. "I can't jump, Jack. I just can't. We're going a friggin' hundred miles an hour. I can't."

"If he gets his hands on us, Sher, it's going to be worse than just being shot, and he's not touching me, Sher… not ever." Jackie's eyes were wide and clear.

"Think of something, Jack," Sheri pleaded. "There has to be a way."

"We have to jump," Jackie repeated. "What the hell else is there?"

Sheri looked down at the floor. "We can derail it…" she said, slowly looking up into Jackie's eyes.

"WHAT?!" Jackie yelled. "YOU'RE NUTS!"

"It's the only way," Sheri concluded.

"Are you nuts?" Jackie exclaimed. "Are you? People could die!"

"No one will die," Sheri insisted. "Maybe a few scrapes, broken bone or two, tops."

Jackie stood eye to eye with her. "Do you have any idea at all how bad… I mean ANY idea how bad what you're suggesting is? We could end up in prison--for the rest of our lives."

"Nah, Jack, didn't you ever see A Few Good Men?"

"Please just shut the hell up," Jackie said nervously, "I think we should just jump when it slows down on one of the curves."

Sheri changed her voice, "*You can't handle the truth.*"

"Stop it, Sher, this isn't a joke."

Sheri threw her hands in the air.

Jackie paced the baggage car floor, shaking her head in disbelief.

"I can't believe I'm doing this," the Conductor said shaking her head. "*Shhhhit.*"

Jackie ran to the rear door that lead back into the train, Sheri right behind her. "Yell into the sleepers that it's an emergency, and to get to the rear of the train. Run through yelling it." Jackie stopped and grabbed Sheri's arm. "Whatever you do --DO NOT go into the coaches--he's back there, Sher."

Sheri quickly nodded, slid the heavy metal door open, and disappeared into the sleepers.

Jackie could hear her yell as she closed the door. She grabbed Sheri's backpack and began taking out anything they couldn't use. She stopped, noting her cigarettes and lighter.

"I should throw these out, turd," she mumbled. "What the hell?" Sheri had two bottles of Cabernet in her other workbag. "I don't wanna know." Jackie said in a half whisper, and placed the bottles into the assistant's backpack and zipped it closed again.

Sliding the loading door the rest of the way open on the Hudson River side of the train, Jackie looked out over the water. It was black and twinkling on the surface in the moonlight. The air was warm and comforting.

"As good a night as any to die, I guess," Jackie whispered.

Sheri returned to the baggage car, out of breath.

"The passengers are gone," the Assistant reported, and then stopped. "But I think our friends are coming."

Jackie's face dropped. "Why?" she asked.

"I raced everyone from the sleepers back toward the coaches; we were just by the café, and all of a sudden, everyone stopped. A guy was yelling 'Did you see the Conducta up there? Answer me, did you see the Conducta? Ya old fuck!' He had a flashlight, Jackie, or at least, someone did."

"That means he does now," Jackie said warily. "We have to get off this train."

"How do you want to do it?" Sheri asked.

"Well," Jackie answered. "If we only unhitch the cars, the train's probably not going to derail; you have the cables, air hoses, and everything else--it'll probably just sputter to a stop…then we're in the middle of the woods with this psycho."

Jackie rubbed her face, smearing dirt and engine grease across her cheek. She continued, "We'll have to bottle the air on the cars and let the engine dump."

"I don't understand," Sheri replied, agitated.

"It's an air-braking system; dumping the air causes the brakes to apply quickly. We're gonna make the brakes apply on the engine--but not the cars."

Sheri looked at her, troubled.

"So, when we separate it," Jackie continued, "the engine will eventually stop, but the rest of it will keep coming, and crash into the engine and derail. Do you understand?" she asked, searching Sheri's face.

"Yeah, but that means we're going to be in the car when it crashes into the engine," Sheri replied, upset.

"It's your idea, Sher," Jackie continued. "I think we should have about twenty seconds to jump."

"Back to jumping," Sheri sighed.

"Hey, look at it this way, Sher… if we survive the derailment, we're ahead of the game. That guy'll be so disoriented, he won't know which way is up."

Sheri nodded uneasily at her.

"I repacked your backpack," Jackie said, rolling her eyes. "That's all you need."

Sheri looked toward the electrical cabinet. "O.K.," she replied quickly.

"So, how do you want to do this?" Jackie asked. "Are you going down or am I?"

"I'll do it," Sheri replied softly.

"Are you sure?" Jackie asked, studying her face.

"Yeah. It's my idea; besides, I was just out there."

"Well, I'm going to find something to wrap your waist," Jackie insisted.

"Why?" Sheri chortled. "So you can drag me on the ground if I fall?"

Jackie was losing her patience. "No, to help secure your balance. Sher, you have to get all the way down to bottle the air."

"I know," Sheri replied chewing on her thumbnail. "So what are you going to use?" she asked, glancing around the car.

"I'll find something," Jackie said, and abruptly jumped up and ran to the rear of the car.

No sooner did Jackie have her back turned than Sheri raced to the opposite end, hurriedly grabbing the black bag from the electrical locker. She quickly ran back and attached it to her backpack, which was lying on the floor of the car and looked at Jackie, who stood holding a rope and looking at her suspiciously.

"What's that?" Jackie asked, trying to focus in on the bag between stretches of moonlight.

"Just stuff we might need," Sheri answered almost casually.

"Good." Jackie nodded as she pulled the rope tightly between her hands, testing its strength. "Are you ready?" she asked as she tied the one-inch rope around Sheri's waist.

"What's the difference?" Sheri said, watching her friend secure the knot.

"The difference is I can go instead."

Sheri didn't look at her; she kept her gaze on the knot.

Jackie studied Sheri's face in the moonlight for a moment, and then looked back down.

"O.K., then," Jackie sighed, satisfied with the knot she had made. She took her conductor's hat off and carefully hung it on a bolt protruding from the metal wall. Sheri rolled her eyes.

The conductor wiped the sweat from her forehead with her arm and started to unbutton her white dress shirt.

"What the hell are you doing, Jackie?"

"Take your shirt off, Sher, there's going to be a lot of wind out there; do you realize how fast we're going? Believe me; you don't want to catch your shirt on anything."

Sheri hastily began unbuttoning her shirt, becoming more aware of the *whoosh, whoosh, whoosh*, and the speed of the train as it thundered over the rails.

"Lookit," Jackie said anxiously as she dropped the shirt and picked the rope back up off the floor. "First you're going to have to bottle the air--the metal angle cock connected to the fat, black air hose--O.K.?"

Sheri dropped her shirt onto the floor next to the Conductor's and nervously tugged on the knot Jackie made around her waist.

"Do you know where I mean?" Jackie's eyes were huge and glowed like burning embers. "The metal handle, Sher."

"Yeah," Sheri replied, agitated, "of course I know where."

"After you bottle it, you have to pull the big metal handle up on the side of the car to uncouple it."

"Listen, Jackie!" Sheri yelled as she walked toward the opening, the conductor on her heels. "I did basic railroading ten years ago."

"Sher…I don't know how fast it's going to uncouple." She hesitated. "I mean, at a steady speed it will stay together, but if we hit a bump or slow down, then speed up --"

"What's your point?" Sheri asked, trying to keep focused.

"I don't know how much time you're going to have to get out of there; it could be minutes… seconds…." She trailed off. "Sheri, you could get killed… crushed."

"Jackie, what's the other option again--we jump at one hundred and twenty miles per hour and are torn to pieces, or we bump the train off the engine and it hopefully knocks us into the water. Your point is?"

"I'm not screwing around, Sher," Jackie warned. "When it parts, this thing's going to be all over the place; you'll get crushed."

"I know, Jack!" Sheri yelled. "Wanna tell me for the tenth time or what?" Sheri stopped, turned around, folded her arms and stared at her.

"Fine," Jackie said, taking a deep breath. "Better get down there, we're running out of time."

The two conductors continued to the opening together and stopped. They stood smiling at one another as though for the last time, their faces red, their eyes filled with the frightened tears of having no choice.

"Look at us," Sheri gave a short, maddened giggle. "Are we having a little Taster's Choice moment here?"

Jackie, standing next to Sheri by the opening, stared down between the steel ends at the ground whizzing by below.

Whoooooooooooosh-   Whoooooooooooosh, Whooooosh, whoosh, whoosh, whoosh.

Sheri turned sideways as the Conductor wrapped the rope around her left hand, letting the slack out as Sheri crossed over onto the engine ledge, about four feet from the ground below and straddled between the massive locomotive and baggage car. Jackie began walking backward toward the huge square opening in the side of the car, careful to keep the rope taut.

The Conductor held on tightly to the long metal bar that ran across the top of the opening. Her heart pounded as she struggled against the pressure of the vacuum created by the speed. It wanted to suck her out. Her hands were sweating as she looked toward the end of the rope--no sign of Sheri.

CHAPTER 12

CRANK-CRANNNK, CRANK, CLAN-AINK.

Jackie spun around toward the other end of the car startled; the giant man in sunglasses was at the door, banging it as he tried to get inside.

"Shit!" she sputtered, looking down again at the ground whizzing by below.

"C'mon, Sher," she murmured, looking through the end of the baggage car door toward the engine. "Damn it." She bit down on her lip and went back to where Sheri had disappeared. She picked up the brakeman's lantern that was lying on the metal floor as she approached the door. She stuck her head outside, between the steel ends, holding the rope tightly and pointing the beam of light down on the river side where Sheri had gone.

"OH NOOO!" SHIT!" Jackie screeched. "NO!" Something had gone wrong. Sheri was hanging onto the engine handle, blood on her arm, her leg under the train through the stirrup on the bottom of the engine ladder.

The train was still thundering over the rails at more than one hundred and twenty miles per hour. Sheri's face was white with fear. Jackie could see that her strength had been sapped.

"SHERI! HANG ON! I'M HERE! I'M HERE!" the Conductor yelled down.

Sheri's head rolled up, and then was jerked back by the force of the wind. She pulled her head forward and half-opened her eyes, the wind causing the lids to flutter and the whites to water uncontrollably.

"My leg--it's caught in the stirrup, I can't move it," Sheri called out weakly.

Gripping the rope tightly around her hands, Jackie quickly glanced back into the car.

"Not good," she hissed frantically. "We're only gonna have one shot at this."

CRAAAANK! CRANK CRANK!

Jackie twisted her head toward the opposite end of the baggage car that led back into the train.

"Sheri--can you move that leg? Can you pull it out of the stirrup?"

Sheri struggled to keep her eyes open. "I think so."

"Pull your leg out and stand up on the stirrup--it's the only way I can get you out."

"My arms are numb," Sheri replied weakly.

"STAND UP! YOU HAVE TO!"

Sheri pulled up on the engine ladder handle, wiggling her arm, trying to get the blood flowing.

CRANK-CRANK-CRANK!

Jackie whipped around toward the opposite end of the baggage car again, shining the light toward the door the henchman was behind, then dropped it onto the floor.

"Stand up!!!" the Conductor yelled. "We're out of time!"

Sheri pulled up on the handle and carefully repositioned her left foot on the stirrup.

"My hands are wet," Sheri yelped, her hair sticking to her pale cheeks and hitting her eyes.

"I've got you, Sheri. I won't let go!"

Jackie quickly undid some of the rope and pulled it over her head and around her back. She wrapped the excess around her wrists until it was taut.

Sheri cried out in pain, pulling her mangled leg through the stirrup, and stood shaking against the side of the engine.

Jackie took a deep breath and stepped across onto the engine ledge, clutching the rope with both hands.

"Sheri! You have to hop up on the top of the stirrup--you have to get to the top of it, I've got no leverage."

Jackie squatted as she straddled, holding the rope tightly, one foot on the baggage car, the other on the engine.

"Hop up! Push up off the stirrup!"

"My hands are wet! I can't," Sheri screamed.

"You have to! Do it!"

Sheri grimaced as she pushed up off the bottom part of the square stirrup. Her foot caught the top edge of the stirrup and slipped. She gasped as her hands slid off the handle and she began to fall between the unforgiving steel ends.

"SHERI!" Jackie screeched as Sheri suddenly swung toward her. Jackie stood quickly and jumped backward, the rope jerked to a stop in the middle of Jackie's back. Sheri screamed in pain as she swung between the cars, her torso crashing into the powerful steel knuckles that hold the baggage car and engine together like Lincoln logs.

"My leg!" Sheri screamed.

Jackie reached down and pulled up on the rope with everything she had. Her face was red, a cold sweat streaming off her forehead.

The Conductor pulled herself into the baggage car and pushed back on the wall with her legs. Her back felt as though it were about to give under the weight. Sheri was grasping at the metal floor trying to pull herself inside. Jackie bent her knees, pulling the slack around her white knuckles and pushed off on the side of the baggage car again, holding the rope tightly.

Sheri grappled at the baggage car ledge as Jackie frantically tugged on the rope.

Sheri got her foot on top of the rubbing steel knuckles that could crush it at any second. She pushed off on it, trying to get inside.

"Push harder, pull yourself in!" Jackie yelled, pulling on the rope, her feet her only leverage.

CRANK CRANK-BAMBAM BAM!

"OPEN THE FUCKIN' DOOR!" the man's muffled voice yelled.

Sheri pushed on the knuckle again and pulled herself halfway into the car. She stopped, gasping for breath.

Jackie yanked the rope a final time and rolled over onto her stomach, grabbing Sheri's scraped arm and pulling her the rest of the way into the car.

Sheri groaned in pain, rolling on her side, her back to Jackie. "My leg, Jackie, my leg--oh-oh, I'm gonna get sick."

Sheri turned her head to the side and threw up. The smell of the coffee-bile mixture made Jackie gag. She looked over at Sheri's leg. Jackie knew from all of the blood that the news wasn't going to be good.

She rose to her knees and rolled Sheri onto her back. Bile and mucus ran from her nose and mouth across her cheek. Sheri coughed and wiped at her mouth, leaving a streak of engine grease in the mix. Her breathing was quick and shallow; Jackie feared she was going into shock.

Jackie rocked back and forth, staring at Sheri as she lay on the dirty floor.

"I have to get us off this train, Sher." Her voice cracked.

CRAAANK! CRAANK!

"I KNOW YOU'RE IN THERE! I KNOW IT!" the man yelled through the door. "THERE'S ONLY ONE WAY OUT, CONDUCTAS--STOP PISSING ME OFF!"

CRAAAAANK-CRANKCRANK-CRANKCRANK-CRAAAAANK!

"OPEN THE DOOR, NOW!"

Jackie looked toward the door; it couldn't be long before he realized the heavy metal entrance could easily be slid open.

Jackie rose to her feet and grabbed Sheri under her arms, gently dragging her across the floor toward the river-side opening. The Conductor quickly grabbed their bags and placed them next to Sheri.

"Jackie—I can't," Sheri groaned in the darkness.

"We have no choice," the Conductor snapped at her assistant and then pulled her closer to the loading door.

She propped Sheri up next to the huge river-side opening on the side of the boxcar as the mammoth train raced over the rails, looked pensively for a moment at her injured assistant, and then closed her eyes.

She reopened them reluctantly, turned, and began to walk toward the engine, tightening her ponytail as she went.

"This is *nuts*, that's what this is," she grumbled, as she took a deep breath and pulled open the boxcar's end door. The wind pushed it past her, smashing it on its hinges against the inside wall of the car. Holding on tightly to the grab iron in the doorway, she looked the short distance across to the back end of the engine and shook her head nervously. Carefully, she crossed her left leg over and straddled between the ledges that separate the locomotive from the train. The wind whipped her face as she brought her other foot forward and stood pressed up against the back of the engine. The *whoosh-whooosh-whoosh* of the train barreling past buildings that she heard from the comfort of the inside of the baggage car was now a loud and intimidating *wisp-wisp-wisp*.

Jackie quickly reached over and tightly gripped the handle on the outside rear corner of the engine. As the train thundered to one hundred and thirty miles per hour, she inched her way over to the corner and lowered herself onto the metal stirrup. Then she locked her right elbow around the handle and reached down, pulling up on the metal uncoupling lever. The pin that ran between the knuckles that held the cars together rose; Jackie's heart skipped a beat, knowing there was definitely no turning back.

She pulled herself up onto the engine ledge quickly and crossed back over into the baggage car. Locating the brakeman's lantern on the floor, she picked it up as she approached, pointing the light at Sheri, then stuffed it quickly into her backpack and slung the bag over her shoulder.

Sheri was still sitting, partially slumped. "You did it," Sheri said with a faint smile.

Jackie quickly took Sheri's work bag and put it over her assistant's shoulder, then stared at her.

The two fell silent. Then their eyes widened as they looked toward the engine.

"*Any second,*" Jackie whispered, terrified. She lunged for the Assistant, grabbing her under the arms and pulling her blood-soaked friend to her feet. She faced Sheri toward the side opening of the baggage car, one arm holding her, the other holding the bar running along the top of it. They were both shaking, looking toward the engine.

"OH SHIT! Breakneck curve, Sher! It's gonna happen! It's gonna happen!"

Jackie bent her legs in a sprint position, ready to push off; Sheri closed her eyes tightly.

"This is crazy!" Sheri yelled. "We're gonna die! We're gonna die!"

Sheri opened her eyes wide and looked toward the engine just as the train hit the curve.

They heard a *PIT-SHEEEEEE!* as the engine broke away and the air hoses broke apart.

"Here it comes, Sher! Get ready!"

They watched in terror as the engine moved away from them, then stopped; the baggage car was now racing toward it and soon slammed back into the engine. The Conductors banged into the edge of the opening and were thrown backward, crashing into the rear of the car as it was lifted into the air.

"What's happening?!" Sheri cried.

"I don't know, I don't know!" Jackie yelled, clutching her shoulder as the car crashed down; they were flung to the opposite side of it.

Water poured in on them as though the car were becoming one with the river. Within seconds they were floating, held now at the front end of the car by the pressure.

"Jackie, help me." Sheri moaned, beginning to sink but refusing to let go of her bags.

Jackie quickly grabbed her around the neck and pulled Sheri and herself along the wall of the car toward where the opening should be. The flow of water stopped; she could now see that the car was tilted at an angle, a partial opening visible, and Jackie tugged Sheri out through it.

The baggage car lay on its side, half submerged in the Hudson River, a small section in the shallows, barely touching the shoreline.

Jackie held Sheri up next to the opening, the boxcar blocking their view of the shore and the derailment. Jackie looked out into the river; part of a castle called Bannerman's was visible. Part of the moat anyway; with small rook-shaped towers that protruded about five feet above the water and stood only about one hundred fifty feet away.

"Sher," Jackie said breathlessly. Sheri rolled her head upright. "I'm going to get us over there." Jackie pointed to Bannerman's through the darkness.

"Why?" Sheri asked, disoriented. "The train's the other way."

"No," Jackie said quietly. "That guy's back there somewhere; I'm not going back there--do you really want to risk it?"

Sheri coughed. "Maybe he's dead."

"And maybe not," Jackie replied nervously. "We can't take that chance."

"Well, what are we going to do over there?" Sheri asked weakly, her face becoming almost ashen. "It's pitch black--decrepit."

"We're going to go there and wait," Jackie answered.

"Why does this sound like the beginning of a Snickers™ commercial?" Sheri coughed.

"I liked you better when you weren't talking." Jackie said breathlessly, looking toward the moat.

"What about my leg, Jackie?" Sheri asked, clenching her teeth and tipping her head back.

"I'll wrap it when we get over there," Jackie offered uneasily, staring at her, conflicted, in the moonlight.

"You're right, we shouldn't go back yet; the pain isn't as bad anymore," Sheri conceded quietly.

"That's because the water's cold; it's numb."

"O.K., Doctor Gupta, whatever. Get me out of here before my skin starts looking like yours," Sheri coughed again.

Jackie bit down on her lip, "You know somethin,' Sher

--Nope, I'm not gonna let you aggravate me right now."

Sheri just nodded, out of breath. Jackie looked at her and tilted her head upright. The Conductor grabbed a scoop of water and tried to wipe the debris from Sheri's face. Her skin was cold, too cold.

"O.K.," Jackie began. "Are you ready?"

"Yeah, I think so." Sheri winced.

"I'm going to pull you across to the moat. We'll rest for a few minutes on one of those towers, then I'll get us over to Bannerman's. Are you sure you're ready?"

"Let's go," Sheri replied weakly.

Jackie took her own backpack, still over her shoulder, and handed it to Sheri. The conductor then let go of the baggage car and got behind her assistant. She put her forearm around Sheri's neck, her foot against the car under the water.

"Let go; just rest your head on my neck."

"Now?"

"Yes, right now," Jackie replied calmly.

Sheri let go and lay back against her, their backpacks on her stomach as Jackie pushed off.

"Listen," Jackie said through huffs as she swam. "I've got you; I'm not going to let you go."

Sheri moaned. "Would you please stop with this *Titanic* crap and get me outta here!"

Jackie clenched her teeth, pushing Sheri's head quickly under the water, then pulling her back up.

Sheri coughed and gave a weak chuckle.

"You are such an idiot," Jackie sighed. Sheri rested her head on Jackie's shoulder, clutching their bags as the Conductor nudged them to the moat, stroke by stroke.

"Here," Jackie said, grabbing Sheri's hand and pulling it onto the rook-shaped tower's window. "Rest." Jackie wiped the hair from Sheri's face.

Sheri looked back toward the train. The center of the engine was on fire; the sleeper cars were in the Hudson. Half the train was derailed, tipped over next to the track. The coaches were upright.

"They're all O.K.," Sheri whispered, relieved.

"What?" Jackie turned her head away from the final stretch to Bannerman's, the castle itself.

"Look," Sheri said, pointing toward the train. "The coaches are upright."

"Doesn't mean anything, Sher. There's major problems over there, trust me." Jackie took a deep breath.

"Are you ready?" Jackie asked.

"I'm ready," Sheri answered.

Jackie grabbed her and began pulling them toward Bannerman's Castle shoreline.

Sheri was facing the train, staring at the engine. She quickly wiped her eyes, trying to make out the silhouette of a large man standing on the shore facing them, his shadow lit by the burning engine. A chill raced through her. She didn't say anything to Jackie.

"This place isn't anywhere near as picturesque at night," Jackie said uneasily as they got closer.

Sheri grinned. "Kinda like what the guys say about you in the morning," Sheri laughed through a garbled cough.

Jackie continued toward the shore. "Ya know something," she said through shallow breaths as she swam, "I'm gonna get you back for this someday, and when I do--it's not gonna be pretty."

Sheri grinned again, holding her head tightly against her conductor's shoulder.

"Not pretty, huh?" Sheri quizzed hoarsely. "Kinda like you before noon?"

The exhausted Conductor grabbed at the shore in the shallows of Bannerman's Island and pulled Sheri up between her legs.

They looked across the river at the derailment in silence. Less than a football field away, they could hear the passengers' chaotic shouts. They sat, dirty, wet and cold, watching.

Sheri couldn't see the man anymore and thought she had imagined it. "You really don't think we should go back there?" she asked quietly as she held her injured leg, gingerly trying to straighten it.

"Stop touching it!" Jackie ordered, grabbing Sheri's hand and pulling it away.

"Stop touching it?" Sheri laughed. "Never mind, I'm not going there." Sheri rolled her head toward Jackie's neck.

"You're nuts," Jackie retorted as she regarded Sheri's leg. The blood was filling the water around it; Jackie could just feel it. "Listen, I have to get that leg on shore."

Sheri let out a yelp. "Jack, it hurts."

"I know, Sher," the Conductor replied calmly. "When I pull you up onto shore, it's not going to feel much better."

"I know," Sheri replied, wincing. "Let's just get it over with, O.K.?"

Jackie stood and grabbed Sheri under her shoulders and began to pull her onto the shore, tripping over a dead branch with a nest of old fishing line wrapped around it. She fell backward over the line, dropping Sheri onto the ground.

"C'MON!" Sheri yelled, "That hurt!"

Jackie yanked the dead branch off the ground and angrily threw it aside. She picked Sheri back up from under her arms and pulled her further onto the dry island.

"Wait a minute," Jackie said, gently resting Sheri on the ground. She grabbed both of the backpacks away from Sheri, reached inside her own bag, took out her pocket knife and brakeman's lantern and then the bottle of wine from Sheri's bag.

"What the hell are you going to do with the knife?" Sheri asked.

"Oh, you have an opener, too?" Jackie retorted, out of breath.

She set the lantern and bottle of wine down on the ground, and picked up her backpack. She knelt down, lifted Sheri's head off of the dead log she was resting it on and positioned the backpack underneath it instead, and then stood, her shoulder aching from getting smacked against the side wall of the baggage car. She then picked up the bottle of wine and holding it between her legs, she reached down and pushed the pocket knife into the cork and turned it again and again. As she pushed the cork down into the Cabernet, the wine squirted up at her face. Sheri lay trembling, looking up at her partner with a grin.

"Don't even say it," Jackie warned. Sheri couldn't stop grinning, despite her pain.

"Now what?" Sheri asked, groaning.

"Drink this; I need you to get drunk," Jackie said, handing her assistant the bottle.

"You sound like my last date."

"Oh, will you stop already and drink the friggin' thing!"

Sheri took the bottle. Jackie watched her drink for a moment and then looked back toward the train. She could see that it was in the water--well, half of it was. She also knew it was only a matter of time before the railroad officials, along with several police agencies, would be down there trying to figure out what had happened and looking for any dead, the survivors, and… *what were they*? Jackie then grabbed Sheri's bad leg and pulled it up onto the log.

"OOUCH!" Sheri cried.

"Shut up, Sher," Jackie murmured, "I have to fix this."

"You can't fix it-OOOOOOOOOOOUCH!" she screamed.

"Shut up," Jackie said, glancing toward the train again. "You're losing too much blood; your pant leg's not just drenched from the water, for crying out loud." Jackie grabbed the brakeman's lantern sitting on the ground beside her and shone the light on Sheri's leg. She cringed as she thought of what she might find underneath her slacks. "We'll figure something out."

"Figure out?" Sheri cried. "You're nuts!"

"We'll figure it out, I said," Jackie repeated sternly. "Just drink."

Sheri took a long gulp, her whole body shivering. "Where's the black plastic bag?" she asked, as she writhed in pain.

"It's right down there," Jackie replied, pointing the light from the brakeman's lantern toward the shore. "Why?"

"There's water in there, that's all," Sheri whispered, as Jackie shone the light on the black bag sitting on the shore.

"I have water," Jackie replied.

She hoped Jackie wouldn't look in the plastic bag, but knew it would only be a matter of time.

Sheri lay looking out over the river. The moonlight reflected off the black water with tiny bursts of white light. She strained to see the train. The engine looked like a large bonfire, not unlike what one might see at any given high school during football season. She didn't try to focus on people, though she could hear them. Nothing too dramatic was going on, maybe a histrionic woman or two, but that was it.

Jackie worriedly contemplated Sheri's oozing wound; she knew it had to be bleeding too much to risk going back into the water.

"After we take care of your leg, we've got to go into that castle," Jackie told Sheri as she glanced around and pointed the brakeman's lantern toward an overgrown stone pathway.

"Why?" Sheri asked defensively. "You don't know who or what the hell is living in there, Jackie."

Jackie rubbed her forehead, aggravated. "I have to make a fire or we're going to freeze tonight."

"So make one here," Sheri huffed.

"Sher--" Jackie said taking a deep, agitated breath. "I don't want to draw attention to this island, plus with the wind coming at us in both directions, it's not going to stay lit anyway." She froze as she looked out into the water. "What's that?" she asked, straining.

"What's WHAT?" Sheri asked, annoyed.

Jackie pointed to one of the towers within the moat they had taken rest on.

"What *is* that?" Jackie asked again, frightened.

Sheri zeroed in on the object, which seemed to be getting closer. "I don't know," she answered with a huff.

"Looks like a soccer ball--buoy maybe?"

"A buoy?" Jackie repeated, contemplating. "Yeah, it's a buoy," she reassured herself.

The Conductor bent down and grabbed a small towel from inside the backpack. "O.K., now let's fix this leg of yours."

Sheri flinched. "Nah, it's fine, Jack, let's just go to the castle."

"Quit it, Sher, it's gonna get infected. Just let me look at it so I can wrap it."

Sheri stared at her fearfully, then reached over and picked up the bottle of red. She took a long drink and lifted it to Jackie.

Jackie reached down, taking the bottle. She looked at it, sighed, and then set it on the ground, steadying it on top of the dead weeds.

She reached under Sheri's head and grabbed a bottle of water from her bag and set it next to the assistant's leg, laying the small towel over her shoulder as she knelt in front of her friend. She gently rolled Sheri's soaking right pants leg over her knee, carefully avoiding the gash.

Jackie closed her eyes, took a deep breath, and looked down at Sheri's leg.

"Well?" Sheri asked, "What's the prognosis, doc?"

Jackie felt the top of Sheri's shin, looking down at it apprehensively.

"I think it's a compound fracture, Sher," Jackie said. "But what I'm worried about is the gash *below* your knee."

"I think I have a band-aid in my bag," Sheri offered.

"Does your ankle hurt at all?" Jackie stalled to buy time as she stared at the oozing wound.

"No," Sheri winced, confused. "That cut, and my knee

--it hurts a lot," Sheri gasped.

"That 'cut' isn't gonna stop bleeding until it's stitched up."

"You're scaring me," Sheri replied, terrified, eyes wide as she searched her conductor's face. "What are you saying--I'm going to lose my leg!?!" she squeaked.

"Oh stop it, would ya," Jackie said annoyed, and shining the brakeman's lantern under Sheri's head into her backpack. "I need string."

"String for what?" Sheri cried.

"I have to stitch it up, Sher; it's not going to stop bleeding on its own."

"YOU'RE GONNA WHAT!!!" Sheri yelled. "Get your hands off of me, don't touch it!"

Jackie sat back on her heels and looked at her friend.

"Here," Jackie said, gently raising Sheri to a sitting position. "I didn't want to do this, but you're making me. Now, look at your leg."

As Sheri looked down, her eyes widened almost cartoonishly. "That's a muscle!" she yelled, petrified. "Is that my muscle?"

Jackie gently lay Sheri back down and stayed sitting on her heels.

"Now, listen: It's not going to stop bleeding, Sher, and I don't know how much blood you've lost… so *you* tell *me*, then." Jackie sat silently, waiting, hands on her knees, looking at Sheri quizzically.

"Well," Sheri began, tears streaming down her cheeks. "How are you going to stitch it up?"

"Let me worry about that and just keep drinking." She stood up and stared at Sheri pointedly. "We don't have morphine…know what I mean?"

Sheri chewed on her thumbnail a moment in silence, taking in the reality, and then put her hands on the ground, pushing herself up to a sitting position. She swiftly grabbed the bottle and began chugging it.

Jackie rummaged through her bag a moment and then picked up the brakeman's lantern. One hand on her hip, she looked around helplessly.

Suddenly, she ran back toward the water and located the fishing line she had tripped over. She grabbed the middle of it and followed it into the bushes. An old, cruddy hook was attached to the end, stuck in a dead branch. Jackie carefully removed the hook and stared at it. Her stomach became queasy. She took the hook and about twenty inches of line and cut the rest away with her pocket knife. She walked back over to Sheri, who was over three-quarters of her way through the bottle.

"O.K.," Jackie said calmly, getting on her knees. She shone the brakeman's lantern into Sheri's backpack and grabbed her lighter. Turning her back, she scrubbed the hook against her pants.

"What are you *doin*'?" Sheri asked, leaning to one side trying to see.

"Just sterilizing the needle," Jackie whispered as she began to burn the hook.

"Needle?" Sheri asked, "Where the hell did you find a needle out here?"

Jackie, back still turned, closed her eyes. She knew the amateur surgery was going to be painful; her heart felt as though it were sinking into an abyss.

"Just finish the wine and lie back," Jackie said calmly, the fishhook black now.

Turning around, she found Sheri lying on her back, the mostly empty bottle of red beside her. Jackie quickly soaked the plastic line in the wine and shook it off.

"Are you ready, Sher?" Jackie asked with a deep breath.

Sheri nodded hesitantly and closed her eyes. Jackie looked down at the gash and shook her head. She grabbed the fishhook by the straight portion and lined up the horseshoe end with the bottom of the gash. Her hands began to shake.

Sheri squirmed around in pain. Jackie knew she was going to scream and quickly grabbed the towel and stuck it in her mouth.

"When you want to scream—" Jackie said patiently, leaning down in front of her, "just bite down on the towel, O.K.?"

Sheri nodded. Jackie cringed as she took a deep breath, looking at the fishhook. She held the speared portion tightly between her thumb and forefinger and pushed it through Sheri's skin, turning the hook and pulling it through.

"JAAAACKEEEE!" Sheri cried, the towel dropping onto the ground.

Jackie pulled up the skin on the opposite side of the gash, punctured it with the fish hook, and pulled the two pieces of flesh together, creating a more orderly oozing, as though having taken an open Ziploc™ bag and closing a small portion on one side.

Sheri arched her back and moaned as Jackie reinserted the hook a second, third, and fourth time. The Conductor turned her head to the side and gagged several times.

"WHAT'S WRONG??!" Sheri cried out in horror. Jackie wiped her mouth with her arm.

"JAAAACKIE!" Sheri cried.

"Almost done—aaaaall moooooost," Jackie said, focusing intently on the wound. Taking the small white towel, her hand still shaking, she poured a little water on it and dabbed the new stitches, gently blotting the blood away. "There you go," she said, and exhaled.

CHAPTER 13

SHWUP-SHWUP-SHWUP, SHWUP-SHWUP-SHWUP.

The two women looked up at the sky. A helicopter with a giant spotlight was flying directly above them, moving toward the derailment site. It hovered briefly over the castle then continued by. Jackie could just make out FBI on its side as it passed.

"Did you see that?" Jackie asked, and continued to dab the wound.

"Yeah," Sheri answered with a groan.

"Do you think it's Mark and Alan?" Jackie asked, dropping the towel.

"You know it's them. Who else?" Sheri moaned.

"They're gonna look for us," Jackie sighed as she put her hands on the ground and plopped down next to Sheri.

"I know that," Sheri said, gazing exhaustedly at the Frankenstein-like stitches, then looking around for the bottle. "What happens if they find us?" Sheri asked her partner weakly.

"How the hell do I know, Sher? Probably nothing good." Jackie looked down at Sheri's leg; she hated to see her in so much pain.

"Thanks, Jack." Sheri slurred, looking cautiously at her leg.

"I love you," Jackie grudgingly muttered, relieved that the wound was no longer bleeding.

"That's what they all say when I'm drunk," Sheri giggled through her buzz. *But, wow.* The only other time Sheri could remember Jackie saying that word, it had been in reference to some idiot getting kicked off the train--"*Loved it.*"

The F.B.I. helicopter landed between the rails fifty feet from the engine on the other side of the river. Jackie and Sheri could see several people jump out and a group of no less than ten passengers quickly swallow them.

They watched the chopper rise back into the air and then head south.

"It's going to be all over the news that we disappeared because of some shady mob dealings we had or something," Jackie said, rubbing her forehead.

"No, it's not," Sheri chided, trying to hide her pain. "More like '*Heroic conductors go away on safari after saving* hundreds of *people*.'" Sheri tried to laugh but could only cough. She covered her mouth, and then looked at her palm. Her eyes widened; she quickly wiped the blood onto the front of her pants.

"Oh, shit." Jackie said and stood up, eyes straining as she faced the shore. "We left the scene of a derailment Sher--we left," she whispered.

"Well, yeah." Sheri replied, throwing her arms in the air. "That *was* the idea." She began to feel nauseated and grabbed the small dying tree next to her in the darkness, trying to stand.

"No," Jackie said worriedly without noticing. "We left, left the scene… left the people--it's over for us." The Conductor trailed off. "There's no going back from this," Jackie continued, looking forlornly at the baggage car in the water. "Ever," she whispered, and then hissed abruptly, "I knew I should never have told you about the house."

"Real nice," Sheri replied defensively, staring at her conductor's back in the darkness. "You're the one who wanted to swim over here; that was your brilliance at work

--remember?" Sheri said, doubling over in pain. "I said no, if you recall."

Jackie continued to stare, conflicted, across the water at the train.

"I know, Sher--just shut up."

"Look at them all," Sheri said incredulously. "There's divers on top of the baggage car already, for Pete's sake."

Jackie stood motionless on the shore, staring at the train, and then pointed the brakeman's lantern onto Sheri's newly stitched leg.

"You lost too much blood, Sher, and that bone is broken. If I bring you back--"

"What?" Sheri mocked weakly. "Bring-me-back-what? So we can lose our jobs in person? C'mon." Sheri wiped her mouth, eyes skyward. "My leg's broken, big deal. Where's your sense of adventure?"

She smiled; Jackie couldn't see the blood in her mouth in the darkness.

"Just c'mon," Sheri said, turning to face the path with the aid of the pathetic tree. "Let's just go up to the castle and make that fire you were babbling about."

Jackie stood silently looking down at the ground.

"Ya know, Jack," Sheri said as she hopped up onto the first uneven step of the path, "when I was little I dreamed of my own castle, too." She looked up the darkened path, then back down toward Jackie. "This wasn't exactly what I had in mind, though." Sheri winked, turned around, and with all the energy she could muster, began hopping up the steps toward the castle.

Jackie looked back guiltily at the train a final time.

"Hey!" Sheri yelled back, hopping further up the path. "There's another bottle of wine in my bag, bring it!"

Jackie shook her head. *Were you shopping for the month or something Sher? Jeeez.*

Jackie wondered if Mark was out there. Hearing Sheri's cough getting further away, she reached into the front zipped section of the backpack and looked at the bottle of wine.

Bending over and picking it up, she gazed at the blackened path. It seemed ominous, and she stood up, lost. Shaking her head, she shone the light onto the ground and picked up her pocket knife. Forcing the cork into the bottle, she turned her head away this time.

"There's no way back from this, Sher," she whispered sadly into the darkness. "W.W.S.D.-- What would Sheri do? Shit, I don't even want to know." she quipped. She picked up a small, dead piece of wood and threw it into the water, watching the odd, circular buoy continue to drift closer to the island. She took a long drink and shivered, and then looked up toward the castle, taking a deep breath.

"I've got your wine, ass!" the Conductor finally yelled and raced up the path into the darkness after her friend. "Oh, man, what am I doing, what-am-I-doing?" Jackie whispered as she bounded the uneven hill. The beam of light from the brakeman's lantern zigzagged on the path as she ran toward the creepy castle.

The fire finally out, Mark stood at the rear of the engine. "What do you make of this?" he asked Alan, who was interviewing people. Mark chipped at the blood on the stirrup.

"One better," Alan replied, handing Mark the Conductors' wet and dirty dress shirts. Marked glanced briefly at the shirts, nodded, then looked again at the stirrup and then up at the knuckle. He walked slowly down to the shoreline, gaze fixed on the baggage car and then, shaking his head, looked across the water toward the dark island.

"What's that?" Mark asked.

"That's Bannerman's Castle," Alan replied matter-of-factly as he walked over and stood next to Mark. "It used to be an arsenal. The guy died in 1918, probably the Spanish flu. He spent around seventeen years building it… amazing, isn't it?"

"Well, what's there now?" Mark asked.

"Nothing, as far as I know," Alan shrugged. "It's protected by the state, I believe, but it's just a broken-down castle."

"Interesting," Mark said, squatting on the shore, contemplating.

A figure stealthily crawled up onto the shore of Bannerman's Island and then stood up in the darkness. His face blank as he reached into his pants pocket and retrieved the small wire. He turned and looked toward the smoking engine, then up the slope toward the castle. He carefully negotiated the overgrown path in the darkness and began to walk up the hill.

Jackie, now close to the castle, slipped as she climbed the steps and fell on her bad shoulder.

"JEEEEEZ!" she yelled, grappling around for the brakeman's lantern, which had flown out of her hand. "What the hell?" she murmured, feeling wetness, and pointed the light at the ground. Her heart pounded. Sheri's blood stained the step. She pointed the light toward the top of the path. Blood was everywhere.

Her eyes widened fearfully, and then she jumped up. "SHERI, I'M COMING!" She ran up the side of the hill, crunching over dead branches and leaves. She stopped, out of breath, as she reached the castle's east-facing wall.

Jackie looked up the side of the nineteenth-century Scottish-inspired castle in the darkness. It was quiet. Too quiet.

"SHERI!" she yelled fearfully, and then hung her head and closed her eyes.

"I'm in here, hag, and you better have my wine!" Sheri called.

Relief washed over Jackie. She ran around to the south-facing wall and walked through the opening caused by deterioration. A green glow stick sat on the ground sixty feet in front of her; there Sheri sat, partially slumped against the west wall. Jackie flashed the light onto the ground. Sheri coughed.

"Be careful, Jack." Sheri said in the darkness. "There's glass all over the place. I cut my arm on a broken bottle."

Jackie rubbed her forehead, a little choked up, and sighed. "Wow, party central, huh?" She approached carefully. "Are you O.K. here?"

"Yeah, this is good, Jack, but I'm cold."

A shiver raced through Jackie's spine.

"I'm gonna make a fire, so hang in there; It's gonna be O.K. Did you grab the lighter?"

"Yeah, did you grab my wine?" Sheri asked. Jackie nodded.

"Was there a sale or something?" Jackie said, looking at her.

"Buy one, get one," Sheri replied, giving a thumbs-up. "C'mon."

Jackie walked toward her. "I'm gonna go get some wood; there's plenty of dead branches out there." The Conductor watched her friend try to get comfortable.

"O.K.," Sheri winced as she took the bottle of Cab from Jackie's hand.

Jackie walked carefully back to the jagged opening.

"Jack—" Sheri called out.

The Conductor stopped and turned back in the darkness.

"Matt liked guys."

"WHAT?" Jackie called back in disbelief.

"That's why I left him, ya know." Sheri coughed. "Can you blame me for not telling you?"

Jackie didn't say a word and walked out onto the overgrown island. She shone the light around the side of the hill, grabbing as many branches as she could find. There was a crackling noise coming from the opposite side. *What the hell is that?* she wondered. Arms full of wood, she struggled to get back to the opening without dropping any. She made her way back over and set the pile in front of Sheri.

"Why did you tell me about Matt?" Jackie quizzed. "You never wanted to tell me before."

Sheri smiled and took another drink, setting the bottle down on the half-stone, half-dirt ground.

"Do you have any idea how humiliating that is?" Sheri asked, tilting her head and looking up at the sky as the clouds shut out the moonlight.

Jackie sighed. "Exactly. So why are you telling me about it now?"

"Because I realized tonight, you're not my friend… you're my sister."

Jackie smiled affectionately.

"I don't mean that literally now, ya know—" Sheri quipped. "I'm not saying your mother *got around* or anything—"

"You are such a complete idiot," Jackie sighed as she placed small pieces of cardboard she'd found between the branches. "I hope we have enough paper to keep this going," Jackie said, concerned, looking up at the darkened sky.

"We have enough paper, don't worry about that," Sheri mumbled.

"What?" Jackie asked looking up at her.

Sheri looked at the bottle, avoiding Jackie's eyes, and took another drink, a mischievous grin spreading across her face.

Jackie sighed, and threw a pebble into the fire. "The black bag?" Jackie asked without looking at her.

"Yep," Sheri grinned, staring into the fire. "And even more behind the mirror in the boiler room at my place."

"Please, I don't want to know." Jackie said, closing her eyes. She sat down and pulled Sheri over to her; Sheri rested her head on Jackie's neck.

"How are you feeling?" Jackie asked, looking into the fire.

"Better," Sheri answered softly. "So what are we gonna do if we can't be conductors anymore?" she asked.

"I can't even think about that, Sher," Jackie answered, choking up. "I'm a conductor, it's who I am."

"Humor me," Sheri prodded. "What else would you do?"

"I don't know; never thought about it," Jackie said, throwing another pebble into the fire.

"C'mon, hag," Sheri prodded, "Somethin' crazy, what would you do?"

Jackie tilted her head, squinted, and looked deeper into the fire.

"I don't know…" She hesitated. "It's hard to imagine not being a conductor; I guess it would have to be something that stemmed from it."

"Like what?" Sheri asked, taking a sip of the wine and lifting the bottle to her. Jackie took it.

"I don't know," she answered, frustrated. "It has to be my choice, though. This, Sher, isn't a choice."

"Well, maybe it's a blessing in disguise," Sheri offered.

"That's a stretch--even for you," Jackie said as she took a drink. "Derailing a fifteen-million dollar train a blessing? I guarantee you, no one would give you a big sloppy kiss for this."

"O.K., so it was crazy—"

"Crazy," Jackie said, and then hesitated. "For starters, yeah."

"O.K.…." Sheri conceded. "But it happened, so now what?"

"You tell me, Sher. It was your brainchild to derail it, and we obviously aren't going to have our jobs anymore."

"Here we go," Sheri complained. "I can't believe you're gonna start blaming me again."

"Well," Jackie said, pushing Sheri up into a sitting position, "I hate to remind you, but this *is* your fault."

"You know something?" Sheri yelled as Jackie stood. "Between what's in *that* bag-- and behind the mirror in the boiler room in my apartment, we could have just started a new life—but *noooo*. Jack, cripes--all you are anymore is that conductor's badge and that friggin' *hell hole* you call a house."

"Oh, go screw yourself, Sher," Jackie hissed as she walked toward the opening.

"Where are you going, Jack?" Sheri asked worriedly.

"I have to get more wood. I'm sure you'll be whining about that next," Jackie said flatly, and walked out into the darkness.

She could hear Sheri grumble "*Ya boring hag,*" as she meandered down the side of the hill and sat on the shore opposite the derailment, looking over at Storm King Mountain in the darkness.

"Sheri, I'm tellin' ya, I'm gonna kill ya," she murmured, tossing small stones and twigs into the river.

Jackie couldn't stay mad at her, though. Sheri, flaws and all, was her best friend. She caught a chill and thought of her sitting up there alone, the fire probably out by now.

With a sigh, she stood up and began to make her way back up the hill, grabbing dead branches as she went.

Sheri sat on the ground, helpless, sipping wine and poking at the dying fires embers with a long twig. She had thrown the green glow stick out into the darkness, lighting up the opening just enough to see when Jackie came back.

"You're such a hag," Sheri sighed. An affectionate smile moved across her lips as she realized that, sooner or later, her friend would return.

Hearing a piece of glass breaking, she quickly looked at the opening, then froze, wide eyed. She could see a head peering inside through the darkness.

The light from the glow stick bounced off his right eye, and what looked like a creepy, red, glowing circle on the left eye. She began to breathe faster, her heart pounding as she watched him walk inside and pick up the glow stick. He moved slowly and calculatingly toward her. Pushing the glow stick into his waistband, he pulled something from his left pocket. Sheri gasped as he came into view. He smiled at her like an angry dog. His reddish glass eye glared at her demonically. She grabbed at the wall, and stood up.

"I have the money..." Sheri stammered, clutching the wall as he slowly came within feet of her.

"I'm past the money now," the henchman growled. He stared down at her as he played with the wire. "I'm going to make this easy on you."

"What?" Sheri asked fearfully, barely able to speak.

He closed his fist and punched her directly on her right temple. Sheri's legs buckled underneath her and she fell backward onto the ground, knocked out cold.

Jackie made it up the hill and walked inside, immediately noticing the silhouette of a man outlined by the green light, and froze, her heart pounding. The Conductor turned off the lantern, placed it on the ground, and then picked up a broken liquor bottle, clenching it as she carefully and quietly approached them. He was kneeling now.

Sheri lay silent on the ground in front of him.

Approaching quietly, Jackie took a quick, shallow breath, lifted the jagged bottle above her head, and then jabbed it into the henchman's back with everything she had.

His hands flew up; she jumped backward as he fell onto the ground with a thud. Disoriented, he tried in vain to grapple for the bottle, and then rolled over on his back. Jackie, breathing erratically, immediately noticed Sheri wasn't moving. Her neck had been cut and blood was running down the front of her shirt.

Enraged, Jackie jumped on the man's chest, straddling him at the waist and bracing herself on her knees as he convulsed violently, then went limp. Trembling, she reached over and grabbed the green glow stick near him on the ground as the fire went out and the interior of the castle went black.

Holding the green light over his face, she noticed blood oozing from the left corner of his mouth as he garbled out his last monstrous breath; his eyes were open. A fake, red-rimmed eye seemed to stare at her from his lifeless body. She shivered and looked over at Sheri. Blood was oozing from her neck and was halfway down the front of her T-shirt now.

"Oh NO!— nononononono," Jackie cried, lifting Sheri's head and gently placing it on her lap. She rocked her back and forth. "It's going to be O.K., Sher," she stammered. "I'm going to get you out of here."

Sheri wasn't moving. Jackie shook her head violently in denial. She closed her eyes tightly for a moment to block out the memory of her father rocking her mother's charred, crunching body, and tears streamed down her face.

Jackie gently rocked Sheri's still body, hands shaking as she looked up at the sky and back down at her best friend—but she was gone.

Jackie turned her head to the side and threw up. Her eyes were so filled with tears, it was as though she were looking at Sheri under water. She couldn't breathe, and her chest was tightening. She stroked Sheri's hair tenderly, minutes had turned to hours before she reluctantly laid her lifeless body down gently on the ground, eyes closed tightly.

After a while, Jackie had finally stopped shaking and, head pressed back against the wall, looked up toward the sky, then over at the opening in the castle wall.

Rising in the darkness, Jackie walked toward the opening. The moon, breaking free from the clouds momentarily, showed her the way. Exiting the castle into the black night, she gasped for air and fell onto the ground. Dazed, she lay there, cold and quiet, staring up at the sky, her eyes puffy and red.

SCHWUP, SCHWUP, SCHWUP-SCHWUP, SCHWUP, SCHWUP.

The conductor lay on her back, watching, heartbroken, as another helicopter passed over. Sitting up, she stared above her at the chopper; then attempted to stand. Wobbly at first, she began to walk, returning to the old, decrepit castle, moving toward Sheri's lifeless body. She couldn't see her and, as she stopped and knelt down, knew she would never see her again.

"I have to go back, Sher," she whispered stoically. "I have to make this right somehow."

The Conductor became nauseated again as she stood and began to walk back out of the castle and down toward the murky river.

Looking out toward the derailment, she could see red and blue lights oscillating across a large swath of the shoreline. People were milling around everywhere.

Wading slowly back into the water, stomach cramping, Jackie began to swim across. Her shoulder aching, she stopped and held onto one of the rook shaped structures in the moat and tried to catch her breath. The thought of her best friend lying in the castle ravaging her with guilt.

She let go and continued swimming toward the baggage car. Suddenly, something grabbed her from under the water. She screamed, then passed out in the diver's arms.

CHAPTER 14

"Jackie, can you hear me?" Mark asked, gently wiping the hair from her eyes. "Jackie-- it's Mark, can you hear me?"

The Conductor finally came to, opening her eyes halfway.

"That's good," Mark whispered. "You're O.K., Jackie, everything's O.K. now."

Jackie sat up, unable to focus completely, her head pounding. "Sheri--" she called out weakly, then fell silent and looked at the ground.

Mark looked at her, concerned.

"What happened to Sheri?" he asked looking down at her.

She looked up at him and then out over the water toward the castle.

"She's in there," Jackie replied, her voice cracking.

"O.K," Mark nodded sympathetically, then glanced at the diver who'd brought Jackie to shore. The diver nodded and headed back into the river. Mark grabbed the radio off his belt.

"Recovery 209," he said calmly into the mic. "Recovery only, white female."

Mark put the radio back on his belt and squatted next to Jackie, who sat shivering, the blue emergency blanket around her shoulders.

"Listen," Mark explained. "I'm going to get you to the hospital, and then I'm going to have to interview you, O.K.?"

Jackie nodded and looked down at the ground. Mark grabbed her chin and tilted it back up toward him.

"We'll clean this up together; for now, just relax--and don't take questions from *anyone*."

Mark whispered to the EMTs standing nearby, and they came and escorted Jackie to the waiting helicopter.

She turned back toward him. "Mark," she called out. He turned around. It's not…I didn't…" she trailed off.

"Relax," Mark said with a nod, then waved *Go* to the EMTs and walked away.

Jackie looked toward Bannerman's a final time.

"Bye, Sher," Jackie whispered, wiping her tears with the corner of the blanket.

She climbed into the chopper; as soon as the EMTs stepped away, two men began shouting behind her.

"We've got the bitch--go, go!"

One of the men jabbed a needle in Jackie's arm, and she passed out on the floor of the chopper, just glimpsing a gun being pointed at the pilot.

"Nitey-nite, Conducta," the gunman chuckled.

Moments later, Mark looked back toward the engine; two of his agents were now lying on the ground groaning.

"What the hell?!?" he yelled.

Alan, who'd been standing a few feet away interviewing people, spun around.

"How the hell did they get in the chopper?" Alan asked, throwing his arms in the air.

"Shhhhit," Mark replied, pulling out his cell phone.

"One-oh-nine's a bachelor, heading north from the derailment--get on it," he barked into the phone. "What? I don't care! Send three from the Albany strip." He closed the cell and looked down at the ground, hands on his hips.

"She's all done," Alan said knowingly, holding his gaze.

Jackie began to come to again. She was trying to open her eyes, but everything looked foggy.

She could hear the *shwup-shwup-shwup* sound, over and over, and men's voices.

The Conductor lay on the floor of the chopper and strained again to see in front of her. She could partially make out three figures facing the other way.

"He said if she don't cough up where it is to just be careful where we dump-ah body," the man in the center said with a chuckle. Jackie's heart pounded.

She blinked several times and looked to her right at the door; her vision was clearing now. She could hear thunder. Looking up front where the men were clustered, she saw windshield wipers flapping; it was pouring out.

"Oh, Sheri," she whispered, panicking. "What do I do?"

"Hey, listen," the man pointing the gun at the pilot said, "believe me, dat broad's gonna talk one way or the otha."

Jackie began to sweat and closed her eyes as the dark-haired man in the middle turned around to look at her.

"I hate haffin' ta do dis to women, though," he said, then turned back toward his buddies. "It's one thing to shoot 'em and get it done, ya know--but torturin' 'ems like… I don't know, beatin' ya motha or somethin'"

"Hey, listen," the man on his right said through a chuckle. "If your *grandmotha* had my half-mil, I'd beat her too."

As they laughed, Jackie inched her way on her back toward the door. She sat up a bit, gazing out the window of the small craft. The Conductor could tell they were following the river. She could see lights on land and blackness beneath them; they weren't that far up; the tree tops seemed close. She stared at the door handle.

Looking out one more time, she lay back on the floor. *It's too big of a drop,* she sulked.

She closed her eyes tightly, trying to find the courage to act.

What would Sheri do? she asked herself, clenching her teeth. *She'd try to fight all of them.*

"I'll tell ya what, though," the guy with the gun said, "I ain't doin' the head this time. Shit gets all over ya like spaghetti." They laughed.

Jackie's eyes opened wide. She sat up and crawled on her knees to the door, yanking at it frantically. The door slid open and before she could think, the wind sucked her out.

She hung onto the sides of the door, dangling over the Hudson. The men were swearing, one leaning out trying to pull the door back to get at her. Jackie looked up at the man who had been standing in the middle, knowing by the crazed look on his face that if she didn't let go now, it wasn't going to end well for her.

Jackie looked down at the enormous, blackened Hudson River, terrified.

She felt a hand grab her arm tightly, holding her in place. She let go with her other hand and began clawing at his arm. She could see the lines of blood form as she dug, and could feel the skin on his arms peeling back under her nails. Abruptly, he let go and she began to fall. Grabbing the skid on the bottom of the chopper tightly, heart pounding, she looked down again.

The water was churning beneath her and she could see the ferocious Troy Dam just ahead.

"OH SHIT!" She screamed and let go of the skid.

Her arms flailed above her head as she tumbled toward the water, hair sticking straight up in the air as though someone were holding it.

The last thing she saw as she broke like a bullet through the surface of the blackened river were the locks, only about one hundred feet away. She shot down many feet into the river, arms flailing above her head. Finally, the pressure stabilized and quickly, ignoring her injured shoulder, she began to swim back up. As she reached the surface, she could feel herself being tugged forward; she gasped for air, searching in front of her, disoriented.

"OHHH, SHIIIIT!" she cried. She was less than fifty feet from the violent water, about to be sucked into the flow pummeling down from the Troy Dam. She swam frantically in the opposite direction, but it was no use. Panic stricken, she oriented herself perpendicular to the falls, facing the Troy side on the southeast, and finally the pull subsided. She swam to shore.

Exhausted, she crawled halfway up onto the shore and lay back in the sludge and dead weeds. The rain poured down on her in the darkness. She sat up and began to cup water in her hands, washing the debris off of her face and hair. She took off her T-shirt and swirled it around in the water, then wrung it out.

Hearing a chopper, she jumped up to run for the tree line, tripping over a metal object sticking out of the ground. She could feel it scrape her shin as she fell. Angrily, she groped behind her blindly. It felt like an angle iron had been pushed into the dirt.

She stood up and yanked it out of the ground, staring at it, and then suddenly dropped to her knees, her face in her hands. "I'm so sorry, Sher," she whispered, out of breath. She lay down on her back; the cool rain drizzled down steadily on top of her. She looked through the branches up at the darkened sky, her heart aching. Each time she closed her eyes she would see Sheri back at Bannerman's, the blood. She rolled onto her side in the mud and weeds, closing her eyes tightly. Her mind went quickly back to the chopper, the fall. She remembered seeing the back of the huge decaying department store building just before plummeting into the river. This was a dangerous place to be at night, by anyone's standards. The last she had read, the homeless and crime rates were three times the national average. *I'll just follow the river back.* Her head felt as though it were spinning, and her eyes started to feel heavy. An image of her father hanging in the shower stall appeared and then she passed out, exhausted.

When a flashlight shone in her eyes a few hours later, she hoisted herself up, dazed, into a sitting position, heart pounding. She let go of the piece of metal to shield them.

"Hey ma'am," the drunken male voice cackled. "You got some change I can borrow from ya's?"

It was still pitch black out. Jackie jerked her head quickly to the left, then to the right, away from the beam of light. She knew she was in trouble. She began to stand up in the mud, acutely aware of the angle iron on the ground next to her.

"No," Jackie replied, taking a deep breath. The light began to bounce; he was scurrying toward her. She reached down calmly and picked the two-foot-long angle iron up off the ground. The light became steady on her again; she stood motionless, glaring at it.

"You ain't goin' no place," the homeless man scowled as he came into view. His face overgrown like the woods they were standing in.

Jackie looked up toward the sky and then back at him. "Do I look like I have money?" she asked hoarsely.

"You better have somethin'!" she could see another light on the ground approaching them.

"Whaja' find?" the gruff male voice called out.

"We gotta girlfriend!" he laughed.

Jackie dropped her T-shirt, and lifted the angle iron as though it were a baseball bat, her eyes glistening in the darkness.

"I'm leaving now, stay back."

"You ain't going no place!" the man yelled again. The second man came up along side of him and moved the light down over Jackie's body, stopping on her bra, her T-shirt on the ground beside her.

"*Damn* nice." the new guy whispered to his friend excitedly. "She looks a little mean, though."

They laughed.

"You get her arms and I'll check her pockets." the first one said as he approached Jackie. As though she didn't hear them; as though it didn't matter if she did. As he came toward her, she squeezed the angle iron with her hand, but her arms had gone numb.

He touched her hair as though it were a rare gem. Frozen, she closed her eyes tightly. The other man, like a cautious, feeble old lion, waited for his cue to join, before approaching the devouring of the gazelle.

Her mind went blank. The first man caressed her wet hair as though entranced by it. Her eyes widened as she watched the second man get closer as though just awakening. She saw it in slow motion as he raised the flashlight and struck her across the face with it. She fell to the ground after the second blow.

Jackie groped around on the ground but there was nothing to grab, nothing to assist. The woods and all of its accessories seemed complicit. She could feel the man who had struck her trying to get his dirty hands into her sopping front pockets. The guy with the hair fetish had turned his attention to her bra and gently tugged on it as though he'd never operated one before.

She pushed herself backward, scratching along the ground. Her pants unzipped, right nipple exposed, suddenly she felt metal above her head. She gently pulled the angle iron closer to her, fingers summoning it into a full grip.

Finally she had the iron knit into her scarred palm. She raised her other arm above her head and clasped it with both hands. As the man leaned his face closer to her breast she took a quick breath and pushed the angle iron down through his neck.

Blood squirted up into her mouth and eyes. She kicked the man who had struck her with the flashlight in the face just as he looked up. As he jumped back up to attack her, she swung the angle iron back around, cracking him across the side of the head. The sound sent a shiver through her spine. She craned her neck to the side as he fell to the ground, her eyes eerily black and shining.

Jackie watched him grope around on the ground for the flashlight. He picked it up and shone the light on his friend's corpse, then on her face. Her eyes glowed in the darkness; the angle iron, held loosely, parallel to her right leg.

"*Give me--the flashlight*," Jackie hissed.

The man saw the other light was at her feet. He stood motionless. The look in her eyes unnerved him. He tossed the light onto the ground.

"*Pick-it-up.*" she said flatly.

Jackie stood glaring at him. He nervously handed her the light.

Walking by without looking at him, she stopped as though hoping he would do something. He didn't.

She entered and walked through the sinister, decaying forest, holding the soaked T-shirt in her left hand, the angle iron in her right. She heard a *shwup-shwup-shwup* and looked up. The helicopter was hovering just above the trees. She quickly hid behind a massive oak. At this point, the letters FBI on the side did nothing to reassure her. The chopper lowered itself, its searchlights shining on the tree line on the opposite side of the river.

Jackie took a deep breath, shivering, and put the soaked T-shirt back on. She stumbled south along the river though the blackened woods toward Sheri's riverside apartment. After a few miles she could see the giant RCA™ dog statue that sat on top of a building across the river and knew she was getting close to Sheri's place.

As she crunched over the dead leaves and branches, she thought she heard a rustling noise. Someone--maybe another homeless person--might be nearby. Her breathing became faster and she began to run.

The moon showed her the holes between trees and she quickly zigzagged through the brush.

An hour later, near Broadway, Sheri's street, Jackie slowed to a walk.

"*Mirror in the boiler room*," she murmured to herself, out of breath. "*Black bag*…. What the hell's in the boiler room, Sher?"

Reaching the apartment, she lifted up the floor mat and grabbed the spare key, opened the door, and quietly walked inside. The place had been ransacked: Couch cut open. Bookshelf broken apart on the floor. Dresser emptied. Clothes, drawers and broken glass everywhere. She swallowed hard, walking through the small apartment surveying the destruction.

Turning around the corner from Sheri's bedroom, she opened the boiler room door. A large mirror hung on the wall; the small nails trying to hold it up were pulled down under its weight.

Carefully, Jackie tried to take the mirror down, but it was stuck. The Conductor yanked on it a bit harder and it ripped off the wall, sheetrock and all.

Jackie stared at the blocks of bills stacked up inside the wall and set the mirror onto the floor.

What do you want me to do with this, Sher? she asked herself uneasily. She walked out of the boiler room, hands on hips. Pursing her lips, she stared at the boiler room door and walked back in, eyes on the blocks of bills.

Suddenly, she heard Sheri's apartment door open. Jackie quickly closed the boiler room door and stood hiding behind it. When she heard Mark's voice, her heart skipped a beat.

"Well, they worked this place over," he said quietly.

"Ya think?" Alan replied sarcastically.

"We better go back to the car and grab the gloves," Mark sighed.

Jackie stood behind the door, heart pounding as their voices got further away.

"Listen," Alan was saying, "all I meant was that birds of a feather flock together--you know that."

"She is not a thief, Alan," Mark replied angrily.

The door slammed shut. Jackie looked hesitantly at the money again. She walked around into the kitchen, grabbed a black trash bag off the floor, and went back to the boiler room.

Throwing the money inside, she jumped up on the loveseat and opened the large, rectangular basement window. She lifted the bag of money and pushed it out the window, then hoisted herself up and crawled outside into the darkness.

Running quickly through the neighbor's yard and around to the front of the house and up the road, she stopped three blocks down and stood still, shivering.

She looked down at the blood on her shirt as a bus approached. Quickly grabbing a handful of dirt and grass, she smudged it over the blood. The bus stopped in front of her; the door made a hissing noise as it opened.

"Please," she said hoarsely to the senior driver. "Please take me up to North Gail--I'll pay you whatever you want." He looked at her battered face and dirty clothes, concerned, then smiled. "It's late… sure."

About twenty minutes later, the bus stopped in front of her driveway and she stepped off.

"I'll just be a minute," she said quietly to the driver.

He winked at her and closed the door. She turned to walk down the driveway and he pulled away. Jackie turned and watched him leave, then stood motionless, staring at the house.

She fished her spare key from the large potted fern and opened the door. It was pitch black and quiet inside. The emptiness she felt smothered her like maggots on a rotten potato.

Turning the light on, she walked through the foyer and into the kitchen. Seating herself at the green stone island, she placed the garbage bag on the counter and stared at it. As she opened it, pulling out a stack of bills, she looked at them, heartbroken.

"You died for nothing, Sher."

The sight of the money before her felt like a knife in her back; the ghosts living in her mind were coming to the surface again.

Now Sheri had been lost to her obsession, too. If it had been she who'd found the money, it would have been given to Lost and Found faster than Michael Jackson would have planned a slumber party. But there it sat in front of her, Lost and Found and going to the cops no longer options.

After a moment she picked up the bag and hid it in the cabinet under the stone island in the center of the kitchen, drawstring hanging out from the cabinet door like any normal trash bag might.

In a daze, she walked up the stairs and stepped into the shower. The smell of the river dripped off her body in soapy orbs as tears mixed with blood and dirt streamed down her face.

As she stepped out, wrapping an oversize green towel around herself, she looked down at her T-shirt on the floor. Blood splotched it as though it were tie-dyed. Eyes closed, she grabbed it and threw it in the wastebasket by the door.

After pulling on blue jeans and a gray sweatshirt and combing her wet hair up into a ponytail, she began to walk back down the stairs.

She was just taking a step when the front door swung open with a crash; she immediately ran back up. There were two of them.

"I'll slit her fuckin' throat—then I'm gonna fuck 'er." They were laughing, maybe drunk. She couldn't tell.

Jackie gasped and tiptoed into her bedroom; the can of pepper spray sat on the dresser. She picked it up quietly and stood behind the door.

"Sounds like your last date," a deep voice laughed.

"Oh fuck you, too."

She heard glass breaking, things being smashed and thrown against the walls. Her heart quickened at the offense as though calling her out to protect her belongings. With each smash, a fist seemed to punch a hole through time within her.

By now it sounded like they were in the den. Biting her lip, she raced down the stairs and into the kitchen. Reaching for the large butcher knife in the block on the counter, she placed the can of pepper spray in her front pocket. One of the men caught her in his peripheral vision.

"What the hell!?!?!" he yelled. "It's her! She's here!"

As he ran toward the kitchen, Jackie peeled toward the downstairs bathroom. One of the men dove at her, grabbing her leg. She dropped onto the floor, swinging the knife at him, but missed, lodging it into the wall.

He jumped back and laughed, standing over her as she panted. As his buddy walked up beside him, she let go of the knife.

He pulled a gun out of his black leather jacket and smiled. "Don't worry, honey, it'll be quick." He held the gun out sideways in front of her, as though presenting it at auction. "There's six in here. We're gonna see how good ya face holds up."

Both men laughed. *They aren't drunk, they're crazy*, Jackie realized.

"C'mon, idiot, we don't have all day," the short, heavy man standing behind him said. The man standing above her tilted his head at her innocently, as if there was nothing abnormal about having a gun pointed at her forehead.

"Now listen: You tell me where the money is and we can maybe forget this ever happened," he said.

Looking into his black eyes, she knew no one would be forgetting anything.

He briefly looked behind him at his buddy. "There's no way she affords this place on a conducta's salary," he cackled as though he were some morbid cross between thug and detective.

She reached into her pocket as the two men casually discussed her pending demise.

"You should do it in the bathroom. Less noise," the heavyset man suggested.

The gunman nodded, bored, and then turned around and leaned down to grab her arm. The fatigue in her arms weighed them down as though they were lead pipes, but her adrenaline won over. She lifted the can of pepper spray, finger firmly on the dispenser button. His eyes opened wide, registering it, just as she sprayed the chemical directly into them.

"FUCK!" he yelled, grabbing at his eyes. He fell to his knees in front of her, face in his hands. She looked up at the other man, breathless. Their eyes locked, and then he abruptly jumped over the injured hit man to get to her.

As she tried to stand, grasping for the wall, he grabbed her arm. She swung the pepper spray can around, dispensing it into his eyes and mouth. He fell to the floor, choking.

Jackie jumped up and ran for the door, grabbing the spare keys to the old Ford pickup that Steve left behind from off its hook, and then raced outside, praying the truck would start. She leaped off the porch and into the pickup. The ignition fired up on cue. Squealing past the Hummer now parked in the driveway, she sped down the mountain.

Her heartbeat stabilized as she pulled into the police station. She sat for a minute, staring at the large blue POLICE sign on the upper portion of the glass door and finally pulled the keys from the ignition.

As she climbed out of the truck, the blue Suburban squealed to a stop in front of the station. She quickly got back inside the truck and shut the door. Mark jumped out of the Suburban's passenger-side door and ran over to her window as the thin, blond sergeant came outside. Jackie rolled down the window an inch.

"Can I help you people?" the sergeant yelled out from the doorway. Mark put his hands on his hips and looked up at the sky for a moment, agitated, and turned around.

"This is an FBI matter, Sergeant," Mark said sternly, holding up his badge. "Go back inside, please."

"*Ohh boy*," the sergeant mocked, and closed the door.

Mark rested his hands on the top of the door frame of Steve's truck and looked in, searching Jackie's face.

"You need to come with us, Jackie," he said softly.

"You almost got me killed," Jackie replied nervously. "Who are you people, anyway?"

He leaned back in the window.

"You don't want to go in there, Jackie. You're opening a huge can of worms here."

"I have to tell them what happened to Sheri," she insisted.

"No one knows anything," Mark said, trying to comfort her.

"But I know."

"You don't understand," Mark said patiently. "We're the only ones who know, and it can stay that way."

"They're in my house, Mark."

Mark stepped back, furrowing his brows.

"Who's in your house?" He shook his head. "Never mind. Lookit, *you're* not in your house and these guys aren't going to sit around eating corn nuts until you get back. They're looking--trust me."

"That's great. Now what do I do?" Jackie threw her hands up, frustrated. "Maybe I should just go find that Jimmy guy myself. No wait, I'll even buy the cement for him."

She lowered her gaze into her lap and placed her hand on her forehead.

"Jimmy will leave you alone," Mark answered firmly.

"Oh, that's convenient. Don't mind if I don't buy into that just yet."

Mark took a deep breath. "He's dead, Jackie. And once we take care of his crew, this will be over."

Jackie glanced quickly up at him. "You killed him?"

"No," Mark replied sternly. "Leave it alone. We have to go."

"Well, what do I do now?" she asked vacantly.

"Come with us until things blow over; then we'll get this squared away with your guys and the National Transportation Safety Board. We'll walk you through what to say."

Jackie tried to hold back her tears, and turned her head away from him, closing her eyes. Mark opened the driver's-side door, gently pulling her out of the seat by her bad arm.

He pulled her to him and held her against his body tightly. She could feel his heart beat, strong and steady.

"It's O.K. now," he whispered. He backed up and lifted her chin. "It's over."

CHAPTER 15

Taking Jackie by the arm, Mark walked her to the Suburban. Numb, Jackie climbed into the backseat. Mark slid in next to her and tapped Alan on the shoulder. Alan nodded and pulled out of the police station parking lot.

As they left, the black Hummer began to follow them. Mark glanced briefly back at it through the double mirror on the door, then looked up and nodded at Alan, who was glancing at him in the rearview.

"Are you thirsty?" Mark asked Jackie casually as he pulled his gun out and changed clips. "You must be." He leaned forward toward Alan. "Let's try to get this done on the bridge."

Alan nodded, eyes transfixed on the Hummer behind them as he drove.

As the Suburban sped over the ramp onto the bridge toward Albany, Mark reached behind the seat into a duffle bag and pulled out an automatic, then handed Jackie a bottle of water. She looked at it and then stared up at Alan's reflection in the rearview; at first he was peering past her, and then met her eyes in the mirror and laughed.

"I hear that," Alan said, then looked through the mirror to the other side at Mark. "It's time, where you want it?"

Jackie jerked around and saw the black Hummer tailgating them. Mark grabbed her arm firmly.

"Face forward," he said robotically, breathing steady. Then he took her hand and smiled at her.

"Ever go hunting?" He handed her the automatic. Jackie began to breathe faster.

"Don't sweat it," Mark reassured. "It's like using a blender. All you do is aim at the bad guys and press the button if I say to—You O.K.?"

Jackie thumped her head back against the seat, and took a deep breath.

"It's going to be O.K., just drown out everything but my voice."

Jackie nodded reluctantly at him. Mark gave her a studious single nod and then looked into the rearview at Alan's eyes.

"NOW," Mark ordered. Alan jerked the wheel left and the Suburban squealed, sliding sideways, stopping on the center of the bridge. The Hummer was stopped two hundred feet behind them. Suddenly the side of the Suburban was pelted by what sounded like corn popping against it. Mark kicked the opposite side door open and grabbed Jackie's hand.

"Gun?" he asked with a whip of his neck in her direction.

"Yeah, I got it," she answered quickly. A few cars driving toward them stopped and U-turned in the center of the bridge and sped away. Mark slid her out onto the ground in front of him.

Alan was already outside. The "corn" continued to pop against the side of the Suburban.

"Alan, cover me!" Mark jumped up and began firing. Jackie held onto the automatic like a pregnant woman with her last French fry. She crouched further down, crawled beneath the Suburban and looked out from underneath the truck as Mark and Alan continued to shoot. Her hands shook as she pointed the gun at the Hummer from under the truck. She closed her eyes and squeezed the trigger: *Bat-bat-bat-bat-bat-batbatbat*. She opened her eyes and looked to her left; Mark's head was tilted sideways, looking in at her.

"Please don't do that again," he asked calmly.

Jackie closed her eyes and began to slide back toward him. Alan yelled just as she heard tires squeal.

"Mark! Get 'er the fuck out of there!"

Mark grabbed Jackie's arm. The Hummer sped toward them as they stood trapped now between the Suburban and the guard rail.

Mark looked over the rail at the river, glanced at the Hummer mere feet from them, and then picked Jackie up and threw her off the bridge.

Just then, the Hummer crashed into the side of the Suburban, pushing it to face forward through the guardrail and halfway off the bridge as Mark and Alan tumbled into the Hudson about fifty feet below.

Jackie was treading in place as Mark swam toward her; Alan was floating behind him, not moving, looking up at the Suburban hanging off the bridge.

"Who the hell was driving that thing?" Mark yelled back to Alan.

Alan looked at him and began to swim toward them.

"It was Jimmy."

Jackie glared at Mark.

"Jimmy, huh?"

Mark clenched his teeth as he bobbed.

"Were not going to do this right now. C'mon."

They swam to the Albany-side shoreline.

The three sat together on the shore, wiping water from their faces, staring up at the Suburban.

Mark pulled the cell phone from his pocket, made a face, and then threw it into the river. Jackie sighed. Alan looked behind them, through the darkened trees and up the embankment.

"C'mon guys," Alan said with a sigh and stood up.

The bullet spun Alan around and he fell to the ground. Mark pushed Jackie back into the water and pulled Alan behind him by the arm, crouching.

Alan pressed his hand against his blood-soaked shoulder.

"Hey ya stupid fucks--where's back-up when ya need it, right!"

They heard men laughing. Jackie's skin crawled as she crouched in the water, the top of her head breaking the surface.

"Jimmy," Alan whispered.

Mark nodded, staring at the outlines of the black trees, unmoving. Leaves began to crunch from different directions. Mark pulled out his Glock, moving behind a nearby tree.

Jackie watched him and stayed in the water; Alan lay just above on the shore. She crawled up toward him.

"Alan," she whispered, "lean toward me."

He wiggled over the ground to her carefully as she reached up and yanked down on his shirtsleeve. Ripping half of it off, she handed it to him.

"Thanks," he whispered, quickly wrapping the material around his arm. "It's O.K.-it just grazed me."

He began to stand, unfastening another gun from a holster on his calf.

Several more shots came at them. Mark dropped to the ground and rattled off three quick rounds.

They could hear something rolling down the hill toward them, crushing over the leaves.

"Ya no-good rat bastards!" a voice yelled, seeming to get closer.

Mark got up into a crouching position and shuffled up the hill a ways, then stopped behind a bush.

The body lay next to him and he looked at the guy. It wasn't Jimmy. *"Shhhhhit," he whispered.*

It was eerily quiet; Jackie's arms were going numb. She crept further up onto the shore as Alan made his way across the shoreline, crouching.

"Stand up, motherfucker."

Jackie froze; the figure was standing about twenty feet away, directly in front of Alan. The Agent slowly rose before him.

There was a quick shuffling sound and then a crunch in the darkness.

"Fuck you," she heard Mark grumble in a low, deep voice, and then, a single shot was fired.

She saw Alan and another guy fall back into the river.

Jackie, breathing fast, looked into the water where the splashing was coming from. She could see only one head, but couldn't tell whose.

"Someone's gotta help me, guys." It was Alan. "Only got one good arm here," he called out stoically, trying to keep his head above the water.

Mark and Jackie quickly jumped in and gently pulled Alan up onto the shore.

"Well, that's gonna give new meaning to 'a shot in the dark.'" Alan laughed breathlessly.

Mark smiled, adrenaline pumping.

"You with us?" Mark said, looking at Jackie.

She nodded, shivering.

"He's dead *now*," Mark noted, and winked at her.

Jackie glanced at him, out of breath.

"Let's get outta here; I'm freezing my balls off," Alan said through a shiver.

The three walked up the dark embankment through the trees and brush, soaked. At the top of the hill, Mark looked up the road at a fluorescent sign reading COORS LIGHT™.

He nodded at Alan and Jackie and they walked down the dark road toward the bar.

A few minutes later they entered the neon-dappled vestibule. Mark asked the twentyish hostess in teenybopper clothes if he could use the phone.

The taxi arrived within minutes; they walked outside. The driver rolled the passenger-side window down.

"Where to?" he asked, smiling and furrowing his brows, amused as he noticed they were all soaking wet.

"North Gail," Mark replied, looking at Jackie.

She looked at Alan, then at the driver. "For two."

Mark looked in her eyes, then at Alan, and nodded at him.

"I could use a beer," Alan said, shaking his head, and walked back into the bar, wringing out his shirt ends as he went.

Jackie and Mark stepped into the cab.

"I'm not even gonna *ask*," the driver said with a throaty chuckle.

"Good," Mark said, looking at him in the rearview, then out the window.

As the cab crossed back over the river and began to twist up through the country roads, Mark rubbed his bottom lip thoughtfully.

"Sheri," he began, without looking at Jackie, and then paused. "It wasn't the derailment, was it?"

"No," Jackie replied quietly, "It was one of the money guys."

Mark nodded.

"And…" he asked, "where might that money guy be now?" He looked over at her. "Whatever you tell me's confidential."

"He's lying inside the castle at Bannerman's…" She hesitated a moment. "With part of a liquor bottle sticking out of his back."

Mark nodded and turned his gaze back out the window.

"You or Sheri?"

"Me."

"And the money?"

She didn't answer.

"Interesting."

"How did this happen," she whispered, looking out the window. Choking up, she closed her eyes.

"There's choices we all make," Mark said, looking at the floor of the cab. "And then, well, sometimes other people make 'em for us--whether we like it or not."

"There's just so much of me missing," she whispered. "You don't understand."

"You know," Mark said, looking at her through the corner of his eye, "my best friend died on the job six years ago, almost to the day."

Jackie looked up at him; he searched her eyes.

"It will never go away, Jackie; you just have to deal with it."

She looked down at the floor of the cab.

"But, ya know, after awhile, believe it or not, the pain will get a little less, a little easier, and life will eventually get back on track--*without her.*"

Mark looked deeper into her eyes, then shrugged and looked out the window. "You just have to find ways to keep her alive."

She looked over at him and sighed. "I'm sorry about your friend."

"I'm sorry about yours."

The taxi pulled into Jackie's darkened driveway.

"Listen, we'll take care of your work. I'm going to bring you inside and make sure you get to sleep."

"I can't sleep," she whispered.

She opened the cab door and took his hand.

Mark gazed at her a moment, then took a deep breath and looked at the roof of the cab. "It's a conflict of interest," he told her softly.

"Not mine." She smiled at him faintly, then let go of his hand. Mark shook his head as she shut the car door.

The cab driver giggled. "Looks pretty cut and dried, if you ask me," he said, raising his eyebrows.

Mark blinked at him in the rearview, sighed, and handed the driver a fifty.

"Did you want me to wait…*awhile*?" the driver asked, pleased with himself.

"No," Mark grumbled, and got out of the car and jogged over to Jackie as she walked up the front steps.

She held her key up to the lock, hands shaking.

Mark put his hand gently over hers and slid the key into the doorknob. He turned her around by the shoulders and tilted her chin up to him.

"It's O.K.," he whispered, and opened the door.

Motioning for her to stay there, he held his hand loosely on top of the gun in his waistband and strode past her into the foyer.

She reached inside and turned the lights on as he zipped through the rooms, then up the stairs, avoiding the broken glass and furniture.

He came back down, nodding at Jackie, who walked gingerly into the house. She felt sick as she looked at the ransacked living room.

Following Mark into the kitchen, she froze as he paused next to the stone island.

"This place is amazing," Mark said, looking around the room.

"Tell me about it," Jackie whispered uneasily, eyeing the tie from the garbage bag hanging out the cabinet door, right next to his thigh. She walked away into the living room and sat on the couch. He followed her.

"Would you like me to make you a fire?" he asked softly from behind her as she sat.

"Fire?" she whispered, dazed. "No, thanks."

He squatted down in front of her.

"Life is going to go on, Jackie," he said, gazing at her with concern. "Pretty soon things will be just like they were before--trust me."

She stared into the empty fireplace.

"Just like before," she murmured.

Mark sighed, looking into her vacant, misty eyes and then stood.

"I'm gonna go get some air," he said, finding himself affected. He turned and began to walk through the living room toward the front door.

Jackie tipped her head back on the couch, looking up at the ceiling, and closed her eyes. Taking a deep breath, she sat up and then stood and walked over to him. She rubbed his back gently as he stood by the door; he clenched his teeth, closed his eyes a moment, then turned to face her. She looked down at his hands, then up into his eyes. They looked smoky and fixed on her.

She could feel herself melt inside; her breathing quickened as the decision only she could make became final. His lips were parted, wet, summoning her.

"I need something," she murmured, the silence of the house overwhelming. She could hear his breathing become thicker as he looked deeper into her eyes, and it made her blush. Gently, she touched his brushed-silver belt buckle, rubbing it with her thumb.

"That's not a problem," he whispered, entranced.

She reached up, slowly sliding her hand over the back of his neck. Moving in closer, she opened her mouth, brushed her tongue slowly between his lips, and then stepped back. Mark reached out and grabbed her around the waist and pulled her up tightly against him. His eyes seemed to look through her. He smiled, conflicted, looked up toward the ceiling uncomfortably a moment, and then back down at her.

Jackie continued to rub the buckle slowly, waiting.

He lifted her chin as she opened her mouth and brushed his tongue across hers, hard and slow. She felt him shiver a moment, then begin to kiss her deeply, passionately, gently pushing her up against the wall. His right hand cupped her breast. He stopped and stepped back.

They stared at one another, breathless.

Mark began to unbutton his shirt, his eyes never leaving hers. She looked down at the buttons, then back up at him, and whispered, "I'm not interested in your shirt."

He looked at her heatedly and then reached out and began to unzip her sweatshirt; she looked down at his fingers and back up at him.

"I'm not interested in my shirt, either."

Eyes twinkling, he reached down and unzipped her jeans; her legs trembling, she undid his belt buckle.

He knelt down, pulling her soaking jeans off one foot at a time, looking up at her. Then he stood, lifting the wet shirt over his head as she unzipped his pants.

He reached into her hair with his right hand and gently tugged her head back, kissing her neck. She held onto his waist breathlessly as he pulled her legs up around him and worked his way into her. She tipped her head back against the wall as he began to take her.

She moaned his name, the ghosts disappearing for a time into his rhythm. She didn't want him to stop. He pushed hard and slow, deeper and deeper inside of her as she gasped with each thrust. It hurt in a way that was incredible. He took his time, and he took her breath away.

When that one particular, inevitable sigh did come, he began gently to back away.

He looked at her and glimpsed the ghosts, the exhaustion, a darker place that he knew all too well, and then placed one arm around her shoulders and the other under her legs and lifted her off the floor. She burrowed her head into his neck, her arms around him as he carried her up the stairs and into the master bathroom. He set her down and she stood looking up at him in silence. He gazed down at her and then reached into the shower stall and turned the water on and adjusted the temperature.

Mark unzipped her sweatshirt the rest of the way and gently stripped it off of her as she stood looking at him, lost. She began to shake as she stepped into the tub, the warm water pouring down over her shivering body. He stepped into the tub behind her, and then turned her around and pulled her up tightly against him.

As he grabbed a bar of soap off of the ceramic-tiled holder on the shower wall with one hand, Jackie stepped back, took the soap, and began to wash his chest. He stood in silence, watching her, as she slowly washed his body, and then her own - her tears camouflaged in the streams of water… but he knew.

Finally, Mark reached behind her and shut the water off. Jackie grabbed two towels as she stepped out, handing one to him and wrapping the other around her waist. She walked into the bedroom and lay down on the bed, on her side looking up at him. The towel now over his shoulder, he sat down beside her for a while, gently stroking her hair and looking into her eyes until she finally closed them. Not a word had been spoken; not a word had to be.

Quietly, he stood and moved toward the bedroom door, picking up Jackie's cordless phone and walking into the hallway.

After hearing him say, "See you out front," she closed her eyes again as he walked back into the room to check on her.

About forty minutes later she could hear a car pull into the driveway and then the front door clicked shut.

"*Sher,*" she murmured, and then fell off to sleep.

CHAPTER 16

Several hours later, the sound of the phone downstairs woke Jackie. She sat up, disoriented, feeling the ghosts return. She walked downstairs to the kitchen; the clock on the stove said eleven o'clock in the morning. She picked up the cordless phone.

"Hello?" she answered in a daze.

"Jackie, hi," the pleasant male voice said. "It's Dave from work. Listen, we talked with the FBI about the derailment. Just wanted you to know you can come back whenever you want." Jackie braved the silence. "You're a hero, you know."

She coiled her head into her neck, incredulous, and dropped the phone onto the counter.

What the hell did you tell these guys, Mark? she asked herself, in disbelief. Walking out onto the front porch, she grabbed the newspaper off the floor.

The bold headline read: CONDUCTOR, 30, DIES IN PASSENGER TRAIN DERAILMENT ON THE HUDSON; RESCUED 200 PASSENGERS.

Jackie walked back inside, in shock. The phone began to ring again; she sighed and answered it. "Hello?"

"Did you see the news?" Mark asked casually.

"I don't feel right about it," Jackie answered, taken aback.

"You'll get over that. Listen, Alan and I went back to the station and picked up your truck, it's out in your driveway."

"I know. Thank you, Mark… for everything," Jackie said, quietly. "I can't believe you did this for me."

"It was pretty amazing, wasn't it," he whispered coyly.

Jackie didn't respond to the flirtation.

"Didn't do it for you," Mark continued. "Did it for the dinner you owe me."

"You think so?" Jackie responded, raising her eyebrows. "And what do you owe *me* for that Jimmy incident?"

"We can work something out," he replied softly.

"Is that so?" Jackie replied quietly.

"Yeah, it is," he murmured, then asked, "Listen, I have a few things to wrap up, can I call you later?"

"That would be great," Jackie answered, then hung up the phone and began to stiffen as she felt the ghosts all around her. She walked into the living room and dropped herself onto the couch. As she sat there, still clutching the newspaper, her skin started to crawl. The house began to feel like an archenemy.

The fire took center stage in her mind. She could see and feel her neighbor throwing her out of the second-floor window, and then her mother's lifeless, charred body crashing down next to her with a *thsp-ch*. A shiver went through her.

"I gotta get out of here," she said, catching a chill. She picked up the phone and called the Dispatcher. "Desk twelve," a woman's voice answered.

"Albany Conductor calling to mark up," Jackie replied stoically. She walked back over to the kitchen as the Dispatcher gave her her assignment.

She looked at the clock above the stainless steel stove again; eleven-thirty.

"Back to work in less than two hours," she replied and hung up. She faced the island, glancing at the cabinet door momentarily, then put down the phone, turned, and walked up the stairs.

Pulling her spare hat off the bedroom closet shelf, she dropped it and watched as it fell onto the floor; she stood staring down at her conductor's badge on the bill.

The Conductor grabbed another uniform off of the hanger in the closet, then pulled on the navy blue pants and buttoned the white dress shirt. Sitting on the end of the bed, she pulled up her black dress socks, staring across the room at her conductor's hat, still sitting there.

Jackie stood and grabbed the Casio off the dresser; the Timex had slipped off somewhere between the derailment and Bannerman's, she was sure. She picked up her conductor's hat and inspected it as she walked out of the room.

Sheri's words haunted her as she descended the stairs.

"They're dead—they're never coming back."

"I know, Sher," the Conductor whispered into the empty foyer. She set her conductor's hat on the cast iron table and walked into the kitchen. "I know."

Reaching into the stone island cabinet, she grabbed the garbage bag and brought it into the living room.

After she unwrapped the stacks of bills, she stared at it all for a moment and then threw it onto the middle of the floor.

Glancing at the headlines on the couch next to her, she picked up the newspaper and rolled it up tightly, as if about to kill a fly.

Still sitting on the table were Sheri's cigarette pack and one of her lighters, left from the other night. Jackie took a cigarette out of the pack, placed it in her mouth, and lit it.

She sat thumbing the lighter as the cigarette smoke swirled in front of her. Her hands started to shake as she took a drag, tears beginning to form in her eyes.

She could see Sheri now; she knew she would come. Ashen, neck open like a Pez dispenser, Sheri was sitting next to her mother's blackened, smiling corpse, forming a gruesome portrait in her mind's eye. Her father's bluish head perched behind them as though posing for this year's Christmas-card photo.

Jackie closed her eyes tightly.

"No," she whispered aloud. "*Please--I can't take it.*" She stubbed out the cigarette.

The lighter still in her shaking hand, she returned to the kitchen.

She stared at the cabinet door below the sink, and then finally opened it. The bottle of refill for the hurricane lamp stared at her.

Walking back to the living room, she stood--lighter in one hand, kerosene in the other--beneath the ten-foot-wide arch, its Roman columns separating the Italian marbled foyer from the pristine cherrywood floors. Tears glistening on her cheeks.

As she regarded the pile of bills on the floor, she took a deep, slow breath and wiped the tears away. The odor of the kerosene dominated the room instantly as she poured it over the pile, making sure to douse some on the couch and the curtains behind it.

She picked the rolled-up newspaper up off the couch, knowing Sheri's spirit could never stand to live as a prisoner there with them. Flicking the lighter off and on, Jackie walked back under the arch, hands shaking, clutching the newspaper.

Trying to blink the tears away, she lit the end of the funneled paper and watched as it quickly ate its way toward her. She had seen that look on a fire before—she had seen it once.

As though a benevolent spirit had taken pity on her, she was suddenly separated from the scene, watching herself from a distance as she threw the flaming arrow onto the floor. The flames mushroomed out over the money and began greedily to consume it.

Jackie walked to the door, feeling the ghosts tugging at her as she came back into her body. Whether to say *help* or *good-bye* she didn't know. But she had, at long last, closed that door to her soul.

Without looking back, she mindlessly grabbed her conductor's hat and walked down the porch steps and into the driveway. She opened the door to the Ford pick-up, stepped inside, and started the engine, her nearest neighbor over a twenty-minute drive away.

Turning it around in the driveway, the fire flickering in her rearview, Jackie took a left onto North Gail and drove down the mountain.

Pulling up at the train station about thirty minutes later, the Conductor pulled the spare ID from around her neck and buzzed herself though the security gates, half expecting to see Sheri pulling in behind her. Rolling through the parking lot, stopping in her regular spot, she sat staring toward the end of the row of spaces to where Sheri's car was still diagonally parked. Finally, she got out of the truck.

She walked alone down the small hill, feeling the hole punched through her heart. As she walked into the crew room, three engineers and six conductors clapped as she passed. Jackie looked down at the floor and hurried by. "Mark," she sighed, and quickly headed into the locker room. Seating herself on the bench against the ceramic-tiled wall, she looked up at the ceiling.

"I can't be a conductor anymore; this isn't right," she said, conflicted.

Maria Summer, a new assistant, walked in on her as she sat, still focused on the ceiling. She stood about five- feet-five, with long, curly black locks reminiscent of one of the characters from the reality show "Jersey Shore." *Cripes*, Jackie snarled, looking over at her.

"Are you O.K.?" Maria asked, scratching her nose. Jackie barely glanced at her.

"Yeah, I'm all right," she answered, and stood up.

"Well, I'm your assistant today," Maria replied, smiling widely.

"O.K.…" Jackie replied, trying to think. It had been so long since she had had to train a newbie. "When they bring the train out, I want you to set it up."

The girl stared blankly; Jackie sighed, then smiled at her. "Just get on the train when they bring it down. I'll meet you out there."

The Assistant's face lit up. "Can I get you a coffee?" she chirped.

"Sure," Jackie replied, even though the thought of it was making her sick to her stomach. The newbie smiled and sauntered out of the locker room. Jackie splashed cold water on her face and walked out into the hall.

Larry Wilcox, an engineer with thirty years' seniority, was standing by the sign-up sheet, eyeing her as she signed up for their train.

"I'm with you today," the Engineer said. Jackie nodded, disinterested. "Did you guys go over a shopping cart or something?" he asked. "Because I can't figure out how that happened."

The conductor looked over at him briefly.

"I don't know what happened, Larry, and I'm not up to spending the day guessing." She could feel her blood pressure rising as he shrugged and walked away from her. Jackie stoically finished writing her name. She walked up the stairs to the Station Master's office and asked for a radio.

"Of course," the salt-and-pepper-haired Station Master said, smiling at her. "Are you up to this?" he asked, concerned, looking in the beat-up locker against the wall for a spare radio. "Because it's no problem. I can take my yard conductor and send him to New York, Jackie."

She looked at him, then smiled. "No, I'm ready," she replied.

"O.K.," he said with a judicious nod. "That's your equipment on the main track; give me a call when you're ready for your passengers," he said, finally handing her a radio.

"Thanks." She went back down the stairs. The talking stopped as she walked by the crews.

"On the main," she called to Larry.

"Right behind you," he yelled after her as she walked out the door.

The Conductor walked up the platform and onto the train. Maria sat in the café, smiling as Jackie plopped her workbag on the table.

"Ready?" Jackie asked. The Assistant nodded fearfully.

"It's a piece of cake," Jackie reassured her. "Follow me."

The Assistant smiled nervously, following her as Jackie explained what setting up the train meant as they walked up through the aisles of the five coaches.

"So you and your assistant were really close, huh?" Maria asked as they stepped off of the train and walked back down the platform toward the rear.

"Yes," Jackie answered indignantly. "But that won't happen again, trust me." She could feel her eyes begin to fill. "You should probably be more concerned about running your train than making friends out here at this point."

"Sorry," the newbie said. "You don't have to be such a hag about it--just asking."

Jackie shook her head and then smiled faintly. "Did you just call me a hag? Too funny." She hesitated a moment, "Don't sweat it," Jackie added, tapping the pouting Assistant on the arm with her radio, and then shifting her eyes away. "Rear of 380 to the head end, over," she called to the Engineer.

"Head end of 380," Larry called back.

"I'm on the point, let's do the brake test," Jackie replied.

"Roger," the Engineer said mechanically. "Three-eighty, setting the brakes."

They finished the brake test; Jackie called the Station Master to send the passengers down.

Soon, Jackie and Maria were standing outside the train, waiting. Suddenly the passengers began bumbling down the platform, weaving in and out, trying to decide which door to get on -- as though it mattered. One of them walked up to Jackie.

"Which way is the train going?" the older woman asked.

"Hopefully, south," Jackie quipped. The Assistant laughed.

"Well, where's south?" the woman asked, throwing her arms in the air. Jackie pointed toward the engine.

"Oh," the woman continued indignantly. "That's all you had to say."

"What the hell?" Maria asked, laughing as the woman walked away.

"You'll get used to them," Jackie assured her. "There's at least one on every trip. Remember, there's no test to ride a train."

The Station Master called on the radio and told them to depart on schedule. Jackie motioned for the Assistant to get on, keyed the coach doors shut, and turned around.

"You can go sit down for now," she told Maria. "I'll take care of the tickets." The Assistant moped her way into the café. When Jackie returned, Maria was sitting, disappointed, at a table.

"O.K., what's wrong now?" Jackie asked, setting her hat onto the table. Maria sat looking out the window, arms folded.

"O.K.," Jackie persisted. "Lay it on me; I know you have questions for me."

Maria's face brightened. "Is it true your husband was cheating--"

"Wait a second," Jackie cut in. "Questions about *the railroad*--not me," she grumbled.

"Oh…sorry," the Assistant apologized.

"Well, this is going to be a long trip, I can see that," Jackie said, looking out the window at the river.

Maria pulled out a newspaper, purposely skipping the derailment article.

"Look at this ring!" Maria said excitedly, turning the paper toward her. Jackie stared bitterly at the solitaire.

"Believe me," the Conductor snarled, "the ring means nothing."

"It's gorgeous!" the Assistant insisted. "The only thing that even comes close to this is emeralds."

Jackie looked at her and sighed. As they pulled alongside the Hudson station platform, Jackie stood up from the table and put her conductor's hat back on.

"Go up and open the front end of the next coach up; we're here."

Maria ran through the car as Jackie strolled out of the café, opened the door and trap stairs and stepped off onto the platform. The Conductor folded her arms across her chest as Maria ignored the people getting on at her door and walked over to her instead.

"Is that a true story about the Hasidics?" she asked, eyes wide.

"What story is that?"

Maria started to talk, but Jackie cut her off, annoyed. "So much for helping the people get on at *your* door, huh?" Jackie asked, staring pointedly at her.

"The Hasidics," the newbie repeated, boldly ignoring the Conductor's quip. "Some of the guys said they travel back and forth on here from the Diamond District in New York City."

"So what?" Jackie replied, losing her patience.

"Do you think they carry diamonds on them?"

Jackie rubbed her forehead. Watching the people board themselves at Maria's door, she blinked slowly at her.

"You-have-to-get-back *ON* now."

"Oh yeah, right!" Maria quickly walked back to her door and up the trap stairs. Jackie shook her head, pulling the radio off her hip.

"Rear of 380 to the head end, over."

"This is the head end of 380, over," Larry answered.

"O.K. to highball Hudson, Lar." Jackie stuck the radio back on her hip and climbed up the trap stairs, then returned to the café and sat back down at a table.

Maria plopped across from her and was about to talk, but saw Jackie's eyes filling with tears as she looked out the window. Maria didn't say another word.

The train began to slow as they approached the derailment site; Jackie's heart pounded. She stared out the window as the train rolled slowly by.

The cars now sat upright on the tracks, yellow tape running completely around them.

White hardhats and safety glasses were everywhere; a gigantic crane pulled at one of the three sleeper cars half-submerged in the water;

one of the men in hardhats was giving hand signals.

Wheel trucks were lined up on the shore. One of the sleepers, a rubble of burnt and twisted metal punched in on its side, sat tipped over next to the rail.

The smell of burnt, molten metal and the sight of the twisted steel as they passed the demolished engine was more than Jackie could bear.

Her red-rimmed eyes guiltily shot a glance at Bannerman's Castle and then closed.

The Conductors finished the trip to New York in silence.

The train finally stopped on the platform and Jackie keyed the doors open. After all the people were off, the two conductors packed their workbags.

"At the end of the trip, in both directions, you have to clear the train," Jackie explained.

Maria stared at her blankly.

"That means that you have to walk through the entire train and make sure no one's sleeping or locked in the bathrooms. It's not a big deal, but you have to do it. We've had people call 911 from the train because they fell asleep and woke up spazzing out when it started moving around the station yard with no one on it."

Maria laughed. "You're not serious, 911…from the *station yard*?"

"Yep," Jackie answered flatly.

"That's too funny!"

"Oh, believe me," Jackie said, brows raised as they stepped off, "it's funny until you start getting questioned about why you didn't clear the train, because they're being sued by some moron who can't keep their iPod™ off until after your announcements."

Maria stopped smiling. "That doesn't happen a lot, does it?"

"Not anymore," Jackie said, looking at her closely. "*Because-we-walk-the-trains*."

Maria followed her up the platform into Penn Station. They walked down the hallway in silence.

"May as well sign up now," Jackie said, looking at her watch. "It's a quick turn today, were outta here at forty-five."

They walked across the hall, signed up for their next train, and crossed back over into the bustling crew room.

Jackie set her bag on the table briefly and then went over the bulletins with the Engineer.

After the job briefing, Jackie walked back over toward the table looking at the track-designation monitor.

"Track five," Jackie said, and slung her workbag over her good shoulder.

"That was fast," the Assistant observed, following her back to the elevators.

Once back on the train, they set their bags down on the café table, put their hats on, and walked out onto the platform. Jackie stood staring at the escalator.

"I'm the bad guy," she murmured. "Mark had it right the first time."

Maria furrowed her brows and looked at her.

"What?" Maria asked, bewildered.

Jackie snapped out of it. "Go set the train up," she ordered.

Maria started to walk away, but the people began rushing down the stairs, then the escalator, heading right for them. She rushed back to Jackie's side.

"Holy shit!" the Assistant giggled. "What's the rush!"

"It's a commuter thing," Jackie answered matter-of-factly. "They come down here every day all week long and wanna get the hell home."

Maria nodded, "I can understand that."

Jackie laughed. "Oh, yeah?" she said, looking at the assistant. "Just wait until you're late--there's nowhere to hide on a train."

Maria uneasily watched the remaining trickle of people hop on.

The woman standing at the top of the escalator gave them the signal to go, and they departed Penn Station.

On the way up the Hudson Run, Jackie looked out the window again at Bannerman's Castle. *I have to keep you alive, Sher,* she thought to herself.

Maria plopped down across from her, laughing. "There's like five of them on here."

"Five what?" Jackie asked, bewildered.

"The Hasidics," Maria squeaked. "Love the braids!"

Jackie stared at her. "Did you get the tickets you were supposed to get?"

Maria's face dropped. "Yeah, I got them," she replied, unsure.

"*Um-hm,*" Jackie said, grabbing them from her hand.

Evening had settled in by the time they pulled up alongside the Albany station platform.

"Hey," Maria began, "I'm meeting some friends at Caroline's tonight; wanna come along?"

"Nah, but thanks," Jackie answered as they came to a stop; she keyed the doors open. Maria was visibly disappointed.

"Listen," Jackie said, mustering a smile. "You did a great job today; go meet your friends, I'll clear the train."

"You don't mind?" the Assistant asked.

"Nah, get outta here."

"Thanks, Jackie."

Jackie flipped a hand at her to go; the Assistant smiled and stepped off the train.

Jackie placed her things back into her workbags just as she had done so many times before. The train was empty and quiet as she began to walk through the coaches, checking each seat for that one confused passenger still remaining.

She walked through the first coach, thinking about what Mark had said as she looked at all of the coffee cups, tiny wine bottles, and hotdog papers stuffed into the seat backs. "Slobs," she whispered.

Someone's glasses case sat on one of the seats. Jackie sighed, picked it up, and continued into the next coach.

By the last set of seats, she noticed a man's blazer up above in the luggage rack. She pulled it down and continued through.

In the final coach, about halfway up on the river side, she saw something black lodged between the armrest and the window. Jackie leaned over and grabbed it.

Wallet? she asked herself. She carried it along with the other items as she finished checking the train.

On her way back through to the café car, the thought of Sheri began to gnaw at her. She rubbed the outside of the black, velvety wallet and stopped in the middle of the last coach before the café. She decided to open it.

She laughed, brows furrowed. "You can't be serious," she said, looking in at the small, clear stones. "*Nah.*"

She remembered back to when Steve had taken her shopping for her engagement ring. He was adamant about not getting ripped off, badgering the jeweler suspiciously about how to tell if the diamond were real and not some piece of "glass junk," as he had put it.

Jackie laughed, recalling how embarrassed she'd been as the snooty jeweler took the diamond and a cubic zirconium, wrote the word IDIOT in small block letters on a piece of paper and then set the stones side by side in front of Steve. He told Steve to hold the cubic just above the print, look through it, and tell him what he saw.

As Steve hovered over the paper with the cubic in hand, the jeweler looked at Jackie and smirked. "Men usually shop for these alone."

"I can read the word through it," Steve had said, handing the jeweler back the stone. Then, with an exaggerated sigh, the jeweler had handed him the diamond.

"Do it again with this one," he stated, bored.

Steve inspected the stone and looked up, brows raised. "No idiot."

Jackie grabbed the *Post* sitting on the seat, picked out one of the large stones, and held it over the newsprint. She repeated the process with several of what had to be at least forty, two- to three-carat stones.

"*Wow*," she murmured.

Jackie zipped the velvety case, set it on the seat, and began to walk away from it. Suddenly, she stopped, turned back around and stood staring down at it. She picked it back up.

"W.W.S.D.," she said, a smile moving over her face.

One of the coach cleaners startled her as he walked inside.

"Oh, I'm sorry," the eighteen-year-old said, "they told me everyone was off the train."

Jackie caressed the velvety material and smiled at him, slapping the pouch twice on the back of the seat.

"Yeah," she said with a nod. "I almost forgot my wallet--almost," she said with a wink, and walked toward the café.

Maria popped her head back in the door as Jackie removed her conductor's hat and placed it slowly on the table.

"Jackie!" she called in to her excitedly. "There's a good-looking guy in a suit outside looking for you!"

Jackie shrugged. "O.K.," she said, zipping the "wallet" into her bag and slinging it over her shoulder, still looking down at her hat pensively. "Tell him I'll be right out."

The Conductor turned and stood looking through the aisles of the coaches for a long moment.

She shook her head and smiled as she stepped off the train and into the warm evening air, her Conductor's hat still sitting in the middle of the table.

-THE END-

Made in the USA
Charleston, SC
07 September 2012